Moonlight Over Muddleford Cove

Kim Nash

Dedication

To my lovely big sis Lisa Jenkins.

Thank you for being my biggest book cheerleader.

This one had to be dedicated to you, bearing in mind that Muddleford is based on Mudeford where we spent lots of time as kids. And don't worry, I didn't tell anyone about when you fell in the water when you were crabbing on Mudeford Quay.

Thanks for loving my books, for sending me pictures of Jack Grealish to cheer me up when I'm feeling down and for sending me hugs in the post.

I promise you the biggest hug in the world when lockdown has finished but I'm warning you that I might cry!

Thanks for being the best big sister I could wish for.

Love you loads.

Your little sis

xxx

Chapter One

A s I STEPPED off the bus, I tutted loudly, realising that I'd left my bag of shopping on the seat. Turning quickly in an effort to get back on, I stumbled and fell into a puddle. I righted myself, reached for the door, and the driver grinned at me as he pulled away. Charming!

Grabbing my handbag, which had also landed in the puddle, I twisted awkwardly and got the heel of my shoe stuck in a drain. The flipping thing wouldn't budge so I took off my shoe and bent down to pull it out. I heaved it out noisily and looked down at my hand. There was a shoe, but in the drain, my heel remained. A group of teenagers who were at the bus stop found it highly amusing, especially when I glared at them. Could this day get any worse?

Chuntering away to myself as I hobbled home, I reflected on my dreadful day. First thing this morning at work, we'd all been called into a meeting to be told that one of our biggest clients had cancelled their contract and it was very serious for the future of Breakspear and Proud. They were the third this month, and the impact of this had meant there'd been talk about jobs being lost. I was the last person employed, and those last in are normally first out. There were lots of hushed whispers around the office and I was really worried.

The work news alone, was a rubbish start, but then the seam at the back of my rather snug-fitting favourite black pencil skirt had split quite spectacularly as I bent over to pick up some papers that Mr Rhodes had dropped on the floor. Everyone in the office had found it highly hilarious that I had huge white pants on, which made it ten times worse when the rest of my outfit was black, so I'd had to tie a cardy around my waist and pop into the only shop for miles around – a small supermarket, with a very basic clothes department, opposite the office – and buy a pair of trousers which weren't cheap and weren't particularly nice either. That's where I'd seen the meal deal for a three course meal for two for twelve pounds and I thought I'd buy it to try to cheer up Callum. He'd been a bit down in the dumps lately and seemed really distant. A treat once in a while wouldn't break the bank. Shame it was still on the bus.

Maybe a night off from talking about our forthcoming wedding would do us both good. There was so much to do, I seemed to be constantly talking about it, and it was doing my head in. We could relax over a nice bottle of Merlot and watch a movie, snuggling up together on the sofa just like the old days. You never knew where it might lead…

I loved the street I lived on. All the houses and tiny front gardens were really well cared for and as I stood at the bottom of our path, and looked up, I felt proud of the painting job I'd done on the front door over the weekend. Now it was a bright glossy red, with a shiny new silver knocker and letterbox in which my dishevelled reflection came back at me. Either side of the front door were artificial potted buxus plants. It was a house that looked loved.

I smoothed down my wayward long brown hair, making a mental note to check my bank account to see if I could afford to get my scraggy split ends trimmed soon, before putting my key in the lock. The front door seemed to be stuck on something, so I gave it a good shove and nearly fell over a suitcase that had been left in the hall. Then my eye caught sight of a bulging holdall on the other side of it. What the hell was this?

Rubbing the back of my neck I yelled, 'Callum, I'm home!'

'Oh God! Nell! Erm! What are you doing here? I wasn't expecting you home yet.' He nervously looked at his watch.

'Dur! I live here!' I grinned and tilted my head to one side. 'Are we having a clear out?'

He couldn't look me in the eye and that was the moment that I knew. My stomach churned.

'We're not, but I am.'

'But, but…' I sank to sit at the bottom of the stairs. 'I don't understand. Where has this come from?'

'I'm sorry, Nell, but I can't do this anymore. I'm leaving.'

And that was when my incredibly crappy day got even crappier.

Chapter Two

BLEEP, BLEEP, BLEEP!
I groaned. I hated the noise of Callum's alarm clock. I went to reach across him to switch it off. I opened my eyes slowly and expected to see Callum lying next to me. And then I remembered that yesterday was the day he'd left me, that it wasn't a dream. Excruciatingly, it hurt all over again. It was a physical ache. Surely, it's your heart that should hurt, not your stomach or even your whole body.

I lay on my back and stared at the purple beaded light fitting, trying to work out what had gone wrong. Yesterday I had been an excited, if a little stressed, fiancée who was getting married in fewer than three months. Today I was single and had no idea what even the next three days held. And what about the future? God only knew about that.

Bleary-eyed from polishing off a bottle of red on my own the night before, I stumbled into the bathroom to grab my slightly grubby towelling pink robe and staggered downstairs, picking up the post from the doormat on the way. All of it was addressed to Callum except for one official-looking white envelope with my name on it, postmarked Dorset.

Crikey, Dorset brought back some memories. It was somewhere I hadn't thought about for years but there had been a time when I considered it with great fondness, a place of wonderful childhood memories. A tiny little bit of my heart flipped over as I remembered some very special people I once knew from there.

Flicking on the kettle, and waiting for it to boil, I ripped open the envelope to see that it was from a Cash and Sons Solicitors asking me to call them. I bit the inside of my cheek, a habit I had when I was nervous, wondering what on earth they wanted with me. I'd ring them at lunchtime and find out.

There was a bit of me that wanted to stay home to nurse my bruised heart, but then the sensible side of me said that I'd be better off keeping busy at work, especially at a time when jobs were in jeopardy. I didn't think a day off right now, despite the reason, would be particularly beneficial to me. I was quite a practical person – I'd had to be with some of the things I'd had to deal with in my life – and decided today shouldn't be an exception.

Peering in the bathroom mirror, I pulled the skin down from the tops of my cheeks and looked at my bloodshot eyes. They were in a state. Callum had always said that my eyes were hazel with flecks of gold and that he loved gazing into them. Huh.

The hot water cascaded over my weary body and scalded my skin as I stood under the shower for way longer than was necessary. A different kind of hurt felt good. I churned over everything in my mind, trying to work out how this had happened and how I hadn't seen it coming. What had I done wrong? I glanced down and saw my skin glowing redder and redder. I knew I couldn't hide in there forever and eventually found my way out. Looking at that blasted alarm clock again, I realised that I needed to crack on if I was going to catch the bus in time to get into the office for 9 a.m.

I grabbed my new trousers off the chair in the bedroom, which was piled high with washing that needed to be put away but never seemed to be, and smoothed the creases out as much as I could. Something Callum had always moaned at me about. One of the many things. He had always told me to hang up my clothes, like he did. But I'd always thought the things that made us different were the things that made us work. We *were* different. He was the yin to my yang.

Callum was an adrenaline junkie, loving nothing more than a weekend spent bungie jumping or extreme mountain biking or white-water rafting, whereas I was the calm one, and a real home bird, someone who liked to read and bake and even crochet from time to time. I realised now those differences that I thought made us special and kept us together were probably what had driven him away.

The weather that morning was damp, drizzly and dreary, which matched my mood perfectly. I looked up at the sky at that horrible fine rain which appears not to be much but gets you soaked through to your skin. It also meant that my hair, which I'd spent ages straightening to look sleek and glossy, would be a frizzy mess within five minutes. God I was miserable.

Resting my head on the bus window, I thought back to when I'd asked Callum last night why he was leaving. He'd sat down on the third stair from the bottom and looked so sad as he'd put his head in his hands and said that he was sorry but he didn't want to live a life where he just existed. He'd said that it wasn't a decision he had taken lightly, but he didn't want to stop at home every night and be a pipe-and-slippers man, growing old when he had his whole life ahead of him. He wanted to go out at night, to the cinema or to pubs and bars, and then he wanted to travel the world and experience different countries and cultures. My idea of experiencing different cultures, he'd said, was having a Chinese or an Indian takeaway on a Saturday night.

He also said that he didn't love me anymore.

Once I was close to work, I could see Shivani to the left of the revolving door which led into the lavish reception for the building. She was taking a drag of her cigarette as if it were the last one she was ever going to be allowed, even though she went down for a fag break at 10.30 a.m. every day. She saw me and threw the butt to the ground, stubbing it out with her shoe, and flung her arms out to me.

'Nell, my love. How are you?' She stood with her hands either side of my arms and rubbed them vigorously, looking deep into my eyes. 'Mmm! You look like crap, so let's pop to the ladies first and see if we can do anything with that face.'

The thing I loved about her the most was how she never fluffed up her words to make anyone feel better.

'And don't worry, I've told everyone at work

what's happened and that you are fine but not to mention it. At least now you can just go and get on with your day without dreading anyone asking you anything.'

Despite her honesty, Shivani was a true diamond who was always putting others before herself. When she wasn't at work, she helped out in a local foodbank. When she wasn't there, she covered the odd shift or two a week at a local women's refuge.

She made me sit on the counter in the ladies loo, while she applied some blusher to my pale cheeks.

'Come on,' she nudged me, passing her mascara over. 'You'll feel better if you look better.'

'Isn't there a rule about using someone else's mascara? I thought I once read that you can pass on mites or something?'

'Oh don't worry, love! It's going straight in the bin after you've used it.'

'I was thinking of me catching yours, actually!'

'Oh, I'm not worried about that.' She smirked. 'There, isn't that better?' She swizzled me around to look in the mirror and I admitted that I did look better than I had when I'd arrived, although that probably wasn't difficult.

'Now you just need to smile.' She poked me in

the ribs and despite me not wanting it to, it did make me laugh.

She always knew how to bring out the best in me and I loved her dearly. I was grateful to her for cheering me up on what I had thought was going to be a very miserable day. I'd thought it possible I might never smile again.

As I sat at my desk, gazing into space, another conversation from the night before came back to me. One where Callum had said that there was nothing I could do and that he had made his decision and wouldn't be changing his mind. Not now and not ever. When I'd asked about all the wedding arrangements that had been made, he told me to cancel them. It was like one gut punch after another.

My mobile rang, startling me from the memory, and I could see on the display that it was Miranda, the wedding organiser from the hotel where we had been going to have our reception. Shivani glanced over at me, and seeing my lip tremble, in her wonderful way, came and took the phone from my hands, where I was staring at it in horror.

'Hi there. This is Shivani here. Nell isn't available right now, so how can I help?'

There was a long pause as Miranda obviously told her the reason for the call.

'I'm so sorry, but there's been a big change in circumstances and the wedding is no longer going ahead. Can you make all the necessary arrangements to make this as easy as you possibly can, please? Nell is, as you can imagine, most distraught at the moment and unable to cope with doing everything herself.'

She winked at me, and despite everything I smiled.

'No point having a dog and barking yourself!' she laughed as she disconnected the call and handed back my phone.

Shivani had a way about her that commanded respect and she told me that Miranda had said that she'd take care of everything she possibly could and would email me in a few days to update me and let me know of any refunds I'd get.

'One less thing for you to worry about right now. Let's head off to the pub at lunchtime and we can grab a sarnie and make a list of everything you have to cancel. I'll help you.'

I could hardly speak the words 'thank you'. I was so grateful to her for taking control. I still felt like a dithering emotional wreck and I wasn't sure everything had quite sunk in yet. I also wished I hadn't drunk all that wine either. I should have known better.

The morning dragged on. I couldn't focus on anything for longer than five minutes at a time but I knew that I was better at work than if I'd been wallowing in self-pity on my own at home. My mum had taught me years ago that there was no point in having a pity party longer than an hour, and that you just had to give yourself a kick up the bum and snap out of it. The advice used to really annoy me when I was younger but it had been helpful throughout my life when I'd been upset about one thing or another. What a shame Mum hadn't taken her own advice.

We'd been through a lot over the years, Mum and I, and this guidance had stood me in good stead. I was only fourteen when Mum and Dad split up, and we moved away, and it was just the two of us against the world. Our small but perfectly formed little family, who had moved to a brand new place where we didn't know a soul. Where we had to make new friends, I had to settle into a new school and Mum had to find a job that could support us both in our new life. And where our life had hit rock bottom.

At 11.30, Mr Rhodes called us all into the conference room. The glass-fronted room overlooked a park and while he was talking to us I was finding it difficult not to concentrate on the couple sitting on a park bench, holding hands, looking as if they were having a very serious conversation. I wondered what they were talking about.

'Nell, did you hear what I said?'

I looked up at him.

'Sorry. Erm, do you mind repeating it? I'm a bit all over the place today.'

'I said, the company is going into liquidation. You'll need to start looking for another job.'

Chapter Three

'SHIT! WHAT THE hell am I going to do now? Not only do I not have a boyfriend, now I don't even have a job.'

Shivani and I had retired to the cosy corner in the Pig and Truffle, which was a stone's throw from the office and a place where we were well known.

'You need to eat something. That's what you are going to do now.' She was properly bossy when the mood took her.

I turned up my nose at the tuna melt sat on the grubby table in front of me and the accompanying chips were swimming in so much fat, it was congealing at the bottom of the bowl. A wave of nausea hit me but I wasn't sure whether it was the situation with Callum, the news that had just been imparted to me and the worry about not having a job, or a hangover from that bottle of red wine I'd necked.

Shivani scrabbled about in her handbag and

magically produced a notebook and a pen.

'We need to make a list. Let's be practical about this situation and recover what we can. So, what do you need to cancel?'

'Well, there's the hotel, but Miranda is going to handle all that. I'll need to go see her, I suppose, and sort everything out face to face.'

'Yes, probably easiest. What about the bridesmaids? You'll have to let them know.'

'Oh god yes. They'll be so disappointed. Ruby was really looking forward to her big day in the limelight. Oh no. Poor Ruby. I adore her. I wonder if they'll stay in touch with me now?' Ruby was Callum's niece; a gorgeous girl, bright and sailing through her first year of high school and, at twelve years old, wise beyond her years. And I loved his sister Sian. Such a lovely woman, the sister I never had. I would miss her so much along with his parents, who were also nice and had taken me under their wing and invited me warmly into their family unit. Maybe we'd stay in touch. Who knew what was the right thing to do in these circumstances?

'You'll have to speak to Callum, you know, and find out what he's doing about telling people. There's no point in you both doing stuff.'

Callum had a huge family and the guest list had

been heavily weighted on his side. The thought of having to tell people was excruciating. How much more embarrassing can it possibly get than having to tell someone that your future husband has changed his mind and actually doesn't want to marry you after all.

'Plus, if they're his family, then he needs to be the one telling them that he's ballsed it all up,' continued Shivani.

'I think if we can make a list first, then perhaps I'll get in touch with Callum and we can go through it and work out who does what. Maybe I'll call him later. I wonder how he is today. Maybe he's regretting what he's done.' My heart began to pound and a tiny bit of hope pierced my heart. 'What if he's having second thoughts?'

The thought of seeing him again, gave me a little flutter in my tummy. Perhaps we could sort all of this out after all. It was all too much. It felt a bit as if my head was going to explode.

Shivani harrumphed.

'What?'

'He's never been good enough for you. He's always seemed to live the life he wanted without considering you at all. Off on his action-packed weekends away with his – supposed – friends.'

'What do you mean "supposed friends"?'

'Well, do you really think that's what he was doing? Remember that time when he told you he was going on a mountain-biking weekend with Phil and then I bumped into Phil in town and Callum told you that Phil had cancelled last minute, so he'd gone with Kev instead?'

'Yes, but that was just unfortunate circumstances.'

'*Really?*' Her raised eyebrow said everything she had on her mind. Then she went back into business mode. 'Flowers?'

'Oh gosh, yes.' I scribbled in the notepad.

'Wedding dress, bridesmaid dresses.'

'Oh my beautiful dress.' A tear escaped my left eye and trickled down my cheek, swiftly followed by another from the other eye. I loved my wedding dress. It had taken weeks for me to find the right one. We'd traipsed around various shops until I'd found it, and the moment I stepped into it, I knew it was 'the one'.

Shivani squeezed my hand and picked at a chip, wincing at the taste.

'It's just a dress, babes.'

I knew she was only trying to make me feel better but what she had said really hurt. It wasn't just a dress, it was my perfect wedding dress which I was going to wear on the most perfect day of my life. The day I was going to marry the love of my life. My Callum. A huge sigh escaped my lips.

'Why do we even come here when the food is so crap?' Shivani threw the chip back in the bowl.

'Well even that's not something we'll have to worry about after the end of the week, is it? We only come here because it's over the road from work. God, this is officially the shittiest week *ever*. And it's only Tuesday.' I rested my head against the back of the armchair and closed my eyes, rubbing my temples in the hope that it might make my headache go away.

'Let's not go back to work this afternoon,' said Shivani. 'Let's stay in the pub and get drunk. It's not like Mr Rhodes can sack us, can he? We're out of a job anyway!' She grabbed the bottle of Pinot Grigio from the ice bucket on the table, and tutted when she saw it was nearly empty. 'Come on, I'll get us another bottle and we'll get this list finished.' She waved the bottle at Will, the barman, who had been working here for over a year. He was handsome in a scruffy way and Shivani really had the hots for him. They had a bit of a thing going on from time to time, but it wasn't really a relationship.

He nodded and said he'd bring another one right over.

'You could always sell stuff on eBay. You said last week that you'd bought your shoes and tiara when you went to town. At least it's a way of getting some of your money back.'

'Suppose so. And there's all those lovely vases I bought for the table decorations and the fairy lights to go inside them, too. I suppose it will help.'

But there was a little bit of me hoping that once I spoke to Callum, and he'd had time to think and had realised what a mistake he'd made, that this would all just be a big blip and everything would be back on. I had to remember to speak to Miranda and tell her not to go ahead with the cancellations before I got chance to speak to Callum. I'd look such a fool if I had to ring again to tell her to put everything back together as it would all be going ahead after all. Whatever would people think?

I groaned as I then thought about the wonderful honeymoon in Barbados we should have been going to the lunchtime after the wedding. I was so looking forward to that and to us getting some quality time away with each other. Maybe we could stall the wedding and go on the honeymoon, spend that time together and see if we could get things back on track. I could make myself do some of those activities that exhilarated Callum so much. We'd already talked about going horse-riding on the beach, but I could really make the effort and be the type of person that he wanted me to be. I'd suggest this when we spoke. My heart lifted a little and a tiny bit of hope surfaced. I could change and be the person he wanted me to be.

Shivani continued on her quest. 'It was the hen party that I was looking forward to the most. A weekend in a spa hotel, would have been just what we need right now to cheer us both up. In fact, that's probably one thing you shouldn't cancel. We'll both deserve that once all this is dealt with.'

She wasn't wrong. A break at a spa couldn't come quick enough.

When the second bottle of Pinot had been emptied, and we couldn't think of anything more to be added to the list – and, to be truthful, I wasn't really that bothered to think of anything more because I was hoping that I could change Callum's mind when we spoke – we decided to call a taxi to take us home. Bugger the expense, I deserved it. Plus I didn't trust myself to get home on a bus in the state I was in.

Shivani popped to the loo while we were waiting for the cab to arrive and I picked up my phone to see if anyone had called. The screen was blank. I glanced at the door to see if Shivani was on her way back and quickly fired off a text. I knew she'd be annoyed with me if she knew what I was doing. Drunk texting was never a good idea.

I miss you. Can we meet tomorrow? We need to talk
xxx

I stared at the phone through bleary eyes for those three little dots that would say he was typing a message back, but they never came. The next time I glanced up, Shivani was leaning across the bar, flashing her cleavage at Will who was lapping up the attention and leaning in as close as he could to her across the bar. Shivani threw her head back with laughter and batted his arm, flirting outrageously. Most of our afternoons at the pub ended like this. Sometimes she went home with Will if it was the end of the night, and then regretted her behaviour the next day and swore that it would never happen again. It was times like that which made me realise how lucky I was to be in a stable, loving relationship. Well, that's what I'd thought at the time.

It appeared that she wasn't going to make that mistake this evening though – plus he was probably working for the rest of the night as it was only just before 7 p.m. – and when she came back over to me, we stumbled outside to wait for the taxi, which soon arrived to take us home. As I walked up the path to my front door, I thought about how much my life had changed in twenty-four hours. I fell on my bed, touching the big gap where Callum had been for the last three years. No fiancé and now no job. What a week this was turning out to be. *And* I was going to have another hangover from hell tomorrow morning.

I checked the phone one final time, in case I'd missed a vitally important text message from Callum declaring his undying love for me and admitting he'd made the biggest mistake ever. When I noticed nothing, I threw it across the room, where instead of it hitting the wall as I had intended it to, it landed on that pile of clean washing that I still hadn't put away.

Still fully clothed, I curled up into the foetal position and cried myself to sleep.

Chapter Four

THE TRING OF a text message coming through woke me and I scrambled across the room to retrieve my phone from the pile of washing it landed on the night before. It was perching precariously on the top of a stretchy pencil skirt, which I threw on the bed before rummaging through the rest of the pile to find a top that went with it. I looked down and realised I was still dressed in the clothes I'd gone to work in the day before and I didn't smell my best. What a scutter.

The name Callum flashed up on my screen and my heart gave a little skip.

Happy to meet. I'll be at Coffee Heaven in Little Ollington at 6 p.m. See you there.

No kisses at the end but perhaps he was embarrassed and didn't know whether to add them or not.

I glanced at the time. It was 8.30 a.m. Crap! I'd obviously slept through the alarm and was going to be late to work. And I needed to make sure that I looked halfway decent to meet Callum on the way home. After the quickest shower in the world, I grabbed a can of dry shampoo, lifted my hair at the roots and sprayed them to disguise the fact that my hair needed attention, and then twisted it up and clipped it on top of my head. As I slipped my feet into my shoes, grabbed my bag and went to run out of the front door, I caught sight of the letter that had arrived yesterday from Cash and Sons. I shoved it in my open handbag and slammed the door behind me.

The bus stop was close to home and I only had to wait a minute for the next bus. Maybe things were going to be on my side today. First Callum texted me, then the bus turned up at the perfect time. They say things happen in threes. I wondered what the third thing could be.

A quick text to Mr Rhodes to say that I had to pop into the doctor's on the way into the office to pick up a prescription, should buy me some time. He wasn't one to delve any further after he once asked Shivani why she'd been off sick and she went into graphic details about her menstrual cycle and he literally turned green before escaping.

I felt more positive today and showed Shivani Callum's message when I got to work.

'Do you think he wants to get back with me?' I asked hopefully.

Her raised eyebrow told me I was living in cloud cuckoo land.

'I think you need to not build up your hopes and just see what he has to say.' She held my hand.

'I don't mean to be cruel Nell, but I don't want you to spend the rest of your day living in hope that he's come to his senses and then have them completely crushed again later if he's adamant the wedding is still off. Just try and get through the day and see what happens later, hey?'

I knew in my heart that what she was saying was right and that she was trying to protect me, but it was still hard to hear. The situation at work wasn't helping either. How were we supposed to throw ourselves into our tasks, when we knew that in a few days the company wouldn't even exist? It seemed so pointless. How could my life be like this when just days ago everything had been perfect?

But had it? I remembered thinking on the bus on the way home on Monday night that I hoped our meal and no wedding talk would cheer Callum up, because he hadn't been himself lately. He'd been working more hours than ever before and had been away to a few conferences, so perhaps in my heart I knew that something wasn't right. Had I been ignoring my intuition?

I popped my phone back in my handbag and my hand brushed the letter from the solicitors. I checked to see whether Mr Rhodes was around, but he seemed to be in discussions in the conference room, so I dialled the number on the top of the letterhead.

The woman who answered practically sung down the phone to me. 'Good morning, thank you for calling Cash and Sons. How may I help you?'

'Morning. My name is Ellen Wagstaff. I received a letter from you in the post, asking for me to contact you.'

'Hold the line please, Miss Wagstaff.'

She sounded most efficient, I'm sure people didn't get that when they called our company. And they certainly wouldn't be now that Mary on reception only had a job till Friday. She was probably telling everyone to bugger off.

A deep male voice was the next thing I heard.

'Good morning, Miss Wagstaff, thank you so much for calling. My name is Dominic Cash. I have some news which I must share with you and I'm sorry to say that it's not all good.'

I had no idea what he was going to come out with. I didn't have a car, so I knew I couldn't have been caught speeding, and I was quite law abiding, so had no idea why I was talking to a solicitor. Even though I knew I'd done nothing wrong, I was feeling particularly wobbly, although that could have been the after effects from necking three bottles of Pinot with my bestie the day before.

'Are you still there, Miss Wagstaff? You've gone awfully quiet.'

'I'm here. What is it?'

'I regret to inform you Miss Wagstaff, that your aunt, Lilian Parsons, passed away recently. I'm sorry to give you this sad news.'

I sat down abruptly. Aunty Lil. I hadn't heard that name for years. Not since Mum had told me that they'd broken all contact when she split up from my dad.

'Oh, Aunty Lil.' A memory of us sitting on the bottom of Aunty Lil's bed in her lovely cosy bedroom came flooding back and I remember dunking Rich Tea biscuits in a cup of tea which was in a china cup and saucer. She always insisted that tea tasted better from china. I racked my brain to see if I could remember how old she would have been. I swallowed a gulp. 'How sad. How?'

'Peacefully, in her sleep. Her dog walker let herself into the house and when she shouted to the dog as she always does, and there was no response, she had a feeling that something was wrong. The doctor said that she'd not been gone for long before she'd been found. The dog was curled up at her feet and she still had a book in her hands, so she'd obviously been reading just before, well, you know...'

I supposed that was some comfort. It must be awful to die alone and in pain. I suppose if you're going to go, in your sleep is as good a way as any. What I couldn't understand, though, was why he was telling me this.

'You're probably wondering why we got in touch with you Miss Wagstaff.'

'No shit, Sherlock!'

'The name is Cash, Miss Wagstaff, not Sherlock.'

Bugger, did I say that out loud? I really needed to think before I opened my mouth. Something else that Callum used to moan at me about. Thinking about it, Callum used to moan at me quite a lot. He also used to moan at me about—

'Miss Wagstaff.' Mr Cash's short sharp tone brought me back to the present. 'You've been named as the sole beneficiary of Lilian Parsons' estate.'

'Oh. Right. Her estate. OK. Thank you for telling me.'

'Can we make an appointment for you to come

in and see me as soon as possible please? We'll need to make arrangements to get everything sorted out.'

'Come and see you? But you're in Dorset.'

He sighed and I heard him mutter under his breath, 'No shit, Sherlock!'

Despite the situation, I giggled.

'Forgive me. Did I say that out loud?' he replied, and the way he said it made me think he was smiling. His voice softened. 'Miss Wagstaff. If you could ring the office when you know when you'll be able to get down here and arrange to come in and see me as soon as you arrive in Dorset we can go through all the official paperwork and get everything sorted out. Don't worry about booking accommodation. When we get your dates, we will sort out everything on your behalf. One less thing for you to worry about. So for now, goodbye, Miss Wagstaff. I look forward to seeing you soon.' The phone went dead.

Good grief, what a shock. Poor Aunty Lil. When I was a young girl I used to spend the whole of the summer holidays with her. She'd lived in a gorgeous house on the coast road in Muddleford in Dorset. It was so different from our two up two down terraced miner's cottage. The two bedrooms on the front of the house had balconies that overlooked the beach and I absolutely loved them. I'd felt like a princess flouncing around in her castle. Mum and Dad came along sometimes, but when they had to work they left me there with Aunty Lil, and I used to spend hours in her perfectly manicured square garden pretending I was an Olympic gymnast, doing cartwheels and ribbon work on the pretend mat.

I never did understand why one day, after she and Dad had split up, Mum said we wouldn't be seeing Aunty Lil again. I'd asked why a few times, but Mum wouldn't discuss it, and I suppose I was so young and wrapped up in a new school and trying to make new friends, discovering a different part of the country, that I shamefully forgot all about Aunty Lil. Today I felt awful that I hadn't given her a second thought for all those years. I wondered what she'd been doing in her life. Whether she'd ever met anyone else. Uncle Alf had died before I was born and she'd been alone all the time I knew her.

She was so kind to me, all the time, but especially when Mum and Dad were going through a particularly bad patch. She used to take me out and treat me, make me feel really special at a time when it felt as if my whole world was going to fall apart.

She was the one who took me to have my ears pierced, much to Mum's horror. I'd been asking her for the whole summer and she'd said no, but when I was staying with Aunty Lil, she said that we should sneak off to get them done and therefore not give Mum the chance to say no. I'd liked her style. She was fun and lovely and it wasn't until I was thinking about her again that I realised I'd missed her in my life and really should have done more about getting in touch with her when I became an adult.

There was more than one very special person I spent time with who lived in Muddleford. That very last summer was incredibly memorable. But after our last night, I'd pushed the memories to the back of my mind, too sad to think about what might have been. I felt a little bit sick, thinking about it now.

When Shivani came back to her desk, I could hardly speak. The memories that had been evoked from the call with the lawyer were totally overwhelming me at a time when my emotions were already a shambled mess. She tried to quiz me but I could hardly string a coherent sentence together and she insisted on yet another lunch at the Pig and Truffle to discuss what on earth the phone call had been about. But this time I was determined I wasn't going to get myself in the state I was in the other evening. I had to meet Callum later and I definitely wanted to look my best. I also had to have my wits about me if I was to persuade him that we were worth taking another chance on and prove to him that I was the one he wanted to spend the rest of his life with.

Chapter Five

TAKING A DEEP breath, I pushed open the door of Coffee Heaven. My mouth was dry and I could feel my heart pounding. I looked around but couldn't see Callum anywhere.

Checking my watch, I realised I was ten minutes early. This time, at least he couldn't have a go at me for being late; another thing about me that annoyed him. That list seemed to be getting longer and longer.

I ordered a skinny latte and took it over to the corner table. I didn't really want everyone listening to our most personal of business.

The owner, Ruth, came over to clean the table next to me. We'd been coming here for a while as their brunches were to die for.

'Evening, lovely, how are you? Where's that gorgeous man of yours? Oh, here he comes now.'

I looked up and there he was. Callum. He'd been my Callum for three whole years. My life, my everything, for those three years.

A memory of the night we met popped into my head. It was in No 12's Wine Bar and I was out on a hen party. My friends were getting very lairy, waving willy balloons around on the dance floor, and I was trying to slope away unnoticed. While I was waiting to get my coat from the cloak room, which was manned by the most incompetent of pervy old men I'd ever met, Callum was waiting to hang his up.

'Heading off are you?' he said.

'I am. I'm rather hoping my friends won't notice for a couple of hours.'

A loud cheer came from the main area and I didn't need to look to see who it had come from. I asked Mr Pervy if he could call me a taxi.

'I'm not your slave you know,' came his grumpy reply.

'You're not her slave, no, but calling this lovely lady a taxi to make sure she gets home safely would be the right thing to do, don't you think? Or would you like me to call the manager, who is my uncle by the way, to ask if this is how you treat your customers these days?'

Mr Pervy immediately swizzled round and dialled a taxi.

'Thank you so much, that was very kind. I hope he doesn't get into trouble with your uncle.'

He winked at me. 'I doubt it, I haven't got a clue who the manager is. But it did the trick, didn't it?'

We laughed. He was handsome, with spiky dark-blond hair, which was clearly covered in hair gel. His eyes were a piercing icy blue that seemed to look straight into my soul.

'I'll wait with you till your taxi arrives. Just to continue my perfect gentleman role.'

'There's really no need, I'll be fine,' I said, though I didn't feel ready to say goodbye to him yet.

'I insist.'

I beamed.

We sat at the bar's outside table and chairs for twenty minutes, chatting like old friends, until the taxi came and he grabbed a receipt from his pocket and asked for my number, which he scribbled down furiously before promising to call the next day. I didn't know if he would or not, but he actually did and the rest, as they say, was history.

Callum smiled at Ruth and slid into the chair opposite me. I was rather hoping he'd sit next to me and had purposely left the chair free of my handbag. Clearly not necessary.

He smiled at me, but it wasn't a smile that reached his eyes. It was more of a forced, pasted-on smile. He cleared his throat formally.

'Nell. How are you?'

'Hi, Callum, I'm OK. Better now I'm seeing you again.' I reached across the table for his hand, which he pulled away.

'Nell. We need to…'

'Callum. Can I just…'

Two people who were so in love not long ago, now couldn't even co-ordinate a conversation. Gosh, this was more awkward than I thought it would be.

'Callum, may I go first, please?'

He nodded.

'I know I've not always been the most perfect of girlfriends. I know that you like excitement and adrenaline-filled activities and I'm more of a home bird, but I'm prepared to change, Callum. I'll do all those things that you wanted me to do. I'll bike up a mountain and then climb down the side it if that's what it takes, and if that's what makes you happy. I'll be tidier around the house. I'll put the washing away every time it comes out of the tumble dryer instead of piling it up on top of the ottoman.' I gave a goofy little smile in the hope that his face would crack, but I was getting nothing back.

'I'll be a better girlfriend, if you'll only give me

a chance, Callum.' I struggled to take a breath. I needed to get everything out while I had the opportunity. 'Let's get married as we planned to and go to Barbados and have a wonderful honeymoon together and I can show you that I can be the person that you want me to be. I love you, Callum. Please…'

He dipped his head and twiddled his thumbs. Seconds felt like hours and he finally looked up at me and deep into my eyes. I loved his eyes, they always melted my heart. God, he was gorgeous and I loved him so much.

'I just don't love you any more, Nell. I'm sorry.'

My heart sank. Nausea swept through my body. My head swam and I thought I was going to pass out. This was exactly what Shivani had been trying to protect me from.

'I'm in love with someone else.'

'*What?*' I couldn't believe what he was saying.

'I'm sorry, Nell, but it's over.'

'I CAN'T HEAR a word you are saying. Calm down, Nell. Where are you?'

'Coffee Heaven. He's gone. Waaaahhhh!'

'I'm on my way.'

Less than fifteen minutes later, Shivani whooshed through the door and headed my way. She slid into the seat next to me and put her arms around me while I broke down once more. Ruth had been sitting on my other side and now patted my arm before standing.

'Can I get you a drink, Shivani?'

Ruth had sat with me for a while but it was getting busy and I knew she really had to go to help behind the counter.

'You'll be OK you know, Nell. You can get through this.'

I wasn't so sure. I told Shivani what had happened through snot filled tears.

'You were right. That weekend he was supposed to be away but you bumped into Phil, he'd actually been away with someone he works with. Fucking Saskia from the marketing department at his work. God, she already sounds like such a stuck-up bitch. How could she start something with someone who was about to get married? What sort of woman does that?'

'I think perhaps you should be turning your aggression on him, babe, not her. You weren't her responsibility. Perhaps she fell in love with him. You can't help who you fall in love with. She might be a really nice person and just fell hard for the wrong man.'

'Oh fuck off, Shivani. Why are you sticking up for her?'

She smiled. I loved that she never took offence, even when I was in my worst of moods. She always saw the good in people.

'There are always two sides to every story, Nell. You only know one side, and knowing Callum, the bit you know is probably only half of his truth. I think you just need to be realistic and work out what happens next. Did you discuss the wedding arrangements with him?'

I showed her the list that I'd made of the things I had agreed to do. Callum had gone away with a list too, though his was way shorter than mine. Typical. He always had played to my better nature, this time spending ages telling me how I was so fabulous at all the admin tasks and that I'd be so much better at it than he was. All he was going to do was tell his family and cancel his and the groomsmen's suit rentals, and the rest was down to me.

I put the list back in my bag and my hand once again brushed past the letter from Cash and Sons. With all the palaver with Callum, it had completely slipped my mind. I wiped away my tears and blew my nose, and told Shivani about the very strange conversation I'd had earlier with the solicitor.

Before I'd even finished talking, she was flicking through her phone finding the easiest way to get to Dorset.

'As you don't drive, it looks like the train is the quickest option. You can get the train from Birmingham to Bournemouth, then there's a bus into Muddleford. There is a coach, but it takes an extra two hours to the train.'

'I just can't take off to Dorset at the drop of a hat.'

'Well, actually, yes you can, and it'll do you good to get away for a few days. It's not like you've got a job to turn up to.'

'Thanks for the reminder. That's something else I really need to think about. I'll never be able to afford the rent on the house without Callum's share. I'll have to sub-let it, or find somewhere cheaper. Although even cheaper is no good if I've got no job. Oh crap, Shivani. What am I going to do?'

'Go to Dorset and find out what the call was all about. It might be just the tonic you need. Get some sea air into your lungs. Get Callum out of your system. Do some thinking while you are there about jobs and where to start looking. Then you can come back and start afresh and work out what the future holds for Nell Wagstaff.'

While there was a part of me that really didn't want to go traipsing all the way to Dorset for a few days, when Shivani worded it like that, there was a tiny bit of me that was starting to feel a little twang of excitement.

Chapter Six

THE SAME DAY the previous week, my life had fallen apart. I hoped this would be a better Monday. I was wondering how long this little mystery stay in Muddleford would last as the train trundled into the station and eventually ground to a halt. A weather-worn 'Welcome to Bournemouth' sign hung at the end of the platform. I took a deep breath, stood, reached up to heave my case from the luggage rack and alighted the train.

A guard gave me directions to the bus station, and I made my way over, wheeling my case behind me, and found the bus to Muddleford. The timetable told me that it should be arriving in just under ten minutes, so the timing was perfect. I had the address of the solicitors' and when I'd rung the office of Cash and Sons, they'd told me the stop to get off at, which was about two hundred and fifty yards away from their offices.

I texted to Shivani as soon as I'd found an empty seat on the bus.

I'm here!

Where's here? Bournemouth? Muddleford? The solicitors?

On the bus to Muddleford. On my way to the solicitors. I feel really nervous.

Oh don't be, you'll be fine. Text me when you can though. Can't wait for an update.

It was only a twenty-minute ride, so the text message exchange and checking my emails on my phone had filled most of the journey. When it was nearly time for me to get off, the driver shouted, 'This is your stop, madam!'

It had been ages since I'd been somewhere new on my own. My life recently had been quite repetitive and mundane. Perhaps that's why Callum had looked elsewhere for something – or should I say *someone* – to fire him up.

Anxiety was getting the better of me. The solicitors had given no indication as to what it was that Aunty Lil had left to me, nor which hotel they'd booked me in to. It would have been nice to go to the hotel to freshen up before the meeting.

Looking at the address in my hand, and correlating it with the brass number above the imposing black door in front of me, I rang the buzzer, not quite sure whether I should push the door or wait.

I pushed. It didn't move. A bleep came through the speaker.

'Good morning, Cash and Sons. How can I help?'

'Hi there, I erm… I have a meeting with Mr Cash at 2 p.m.'

'Oh you must be Miss Wagstaff. Do come in.' A click indicated that this time when I pushed the door, it would open.

'Good morning. I'm Sally. I do hope you had a good journey down.' The pretty receptionist smiled sweetly at me. 'Can I get you a tea or a coffee at all? Or a glass of water maybe?'

'Oh, I'm gagging for a coffee if you don't mind.' I could have kicked myself for being so immediately familiar. I needed to remember where I was.

'Miss Wagstaff. It's so nice to meet you finally.' A tall slim man in a navy-blue suit which looked like it needed a good pressing, white shirt and a grey spotty tie with a matching hanky, emerged from a side door and reached out to shake my hand. 'Let me take your case. Sally will bring our drinks through. We may as well make a start if that's OK with you. We have a lot to get through.'

Frowning, I followed him through into his office, which was exactly how I had expected it to look. Dark-wood furniture, shelves full of academic books, and a leather chesterfield chair sat opposite a huge dark-wood desk with a brass light on the corner.

Mr Cash sat and tucked his chair under his side of the desk and linked his hands together, resting them on the desk in front of him. He didn't look as old as I had first thought, seeing him closer.

'So, firstly, once again, I'd like to offer you our condolences on the death of your aunt. As I said, you are the sole beneficiary of Mrs Lilian Parsons. Congratulations. How does that feel?'

'OK I guess. A surprise, as I'd said on the phone.'

'I can only imagine. We were very fond of Lilian. We've dealt with her personal matters as solicitors for many years, first my father before he retired and then me. Now, you are probably wondering what exactly you've inherited, aren't you?'

I nodded but didn't want to seem mercenary.

He opened a manilla folder and started to read. In my head, I'd been thinking maybe it was one of those huge diamond rings that she used to wear that always glittered away beautifully when it caught the light. She always let me try on her rings, and we joked about it and she said that she'd leave them to me. If I'd inherited one of those I'd be chuffed to bits.

'So, you have inherited 37 Larkspur Lane in Muddleford. Here are the keys. All of the contents of the house will be yours too, just to be clear.' He pushed forward a large bunch of keys held together with a silver dog keyring.

I looked down at them and then up at him in astonishment. I went to speak but he held his hand up to silence me.

'And these are to number 136 beach hut on Muddleford Beach.'

I raised my eyebrows as another set of keys crossed the desk.

'This final set of keys is to Lilian's car, which I have been told is parked in the garage at the property.'

I was struggling to take it all in. She'd left her house to me, a beach hut *and* her car. A giggle escaped my lips as I envisaged an old-lady car and Aunty Lil being chauffeured like in *Driving Miss Daisy*. Funny how out of that list of things, the car was the one thing that stuck out.

'And finally, Miss Wagstaff, the monetary sum of £350,000.'

'I'm sorry. For a minute there I thought you said £350,000. Could you repeat that, please?'

'Yes, that's exactly what I said. £350,000.'

'Oh my god! Seriously? How the hell did Aunty Lilian have that sort of money? And if she did, why on earth didn't she spend it on herself?'

'Oh, please don't worry. I can assure you that Lilian had a very nice life and spent everything she wanted to. She made some very sound investments over the years. I realise this is quite a lot for you to take in. We have provisionally booked you into a hotel for the next few days, but we also thought there may be a possibility that you might like to stay at the property. Entirely your decision, but if you could let me know which you'd prefer I can let Sally get in touch with the hotel to confirm or cancel the booking.'

'I can't believe it. I really can't.'

'I do have a letter for you from Lilian that she asked me to pass on to you following the event of her death. I'm going to pop out of the room and leave you in private to read it. I'll chivvy along that coffee while I'm out.'

An envelope appeared in front of me on the edge of the desk.

Mr Cash rested his hand on my shoulder as he passed by and he smiled as I looked up at him, still totally discombobulated.

With trembling hands, I ripped open the envelope, took out the letter and smoothed it down.

My dearest Nell,

I'm sorry if this letter and news has come as somewhat of a shock to you. Some of the fondest and most treasured memories in my life are of you, my darling girl. Those summers we spent together were very special and they meant the absolute world to me.

I'm not sure if you ever knew that I had a daughter, Sophia. She was the most beautiful, sweet, golden little girl who was the absolute and utter love of my life. Sadly, and it still pains me today to say these words, but when she was six months old she became ill and I was totally and utterly devastated when her beautiful life ended. We tried again a few months on, but my heart was so badly broken that I didn't really want to go through it all again, and when the doctor confirmed that they had discovered that I couldn't bear children from the complications in my first pregnancy, there was a little bit of me that was relieved. How could I ever have replaced my beautiful girl?

I suffered from severe depression for many years, sometimes staying in bed for days on end. I lived in a bubble of sadness, refusing to accept my life the way it was. Nothing and nobody could give me what I wanted, which was my darling Sophia back in my life to watch her grow up. I felt our futures had been cruelly stolen from us. In my darkest of days I considered taking my own life, all I wanted was to be with my daughter whatever that meant.

It was you, my beautiful Nell, who saved me, when I felt as if I had nothing to live for. Those summers that you came to stay made me feel that life was finally worth living again. In your presence, I could once more see the colours of the flowers in the garden and smell the salty sea air. The world came back to life. And it was because of you, that I thought about my daughter again, with love and wonder for what Sophia might have been like and how our lives might have been, and gratitude for the short time that I did hold her in my arms. You'll never know how you saved me.

When your mum and dad parted company, I was sad again and hurt. Your mother said some very cruel things to me and I behaved rashly and told her to leave and that I never wanted to see her again. What I didn't bargain for was that she took me literally and from that day I saw neither of you ever again.

Once again, I had to make a new life for myself and I did exactly that. You had given me the will to live again, and to live my best life. I owed it to Sophia and I owed it to you. I had a wonderful life and I was lucky that I had love in my life in many different way. Not everyone does. I hope that you are loved by someone, my Nell. You deserve to be. And if you are not, I hope you will find your one true love.

When I met Norman for the first time, I fell immediately head over heels. I loved him more than I thought I was capable of loving again. I'm sure you will be meeting Norman very soon. I hope that, in time, you become fond of him too.

Take the money, take the properties and do with them whatever you wish. I trust you to make the decision that is right for you. You gave me my life back, and now I'm giving you a head start in yours.

Live your life with love and passion and be brave! Don't save things for best. Today is good enough. Eat from the best crockery, pour your tea from a pot into the best china, drink gin from cut glasses, wear your *best clothes today. You deserve the very best of everything. Tomorrow is never promised, my love, so live life for today.*

Goodbye, my love, and I hope you think of me from time to time with fondness. I will be forever grateful for what you gave to me.

With much love.
Your Aunty Lil xxx

Chapter Seven

A SUBTLE COUGH, brought me back to the room. Mr Cash was standing in the doorway.

'So, Miss Wagstaff, have you got any thoughts yet? Would you like to go straight to the house, or check in at the hotel? Or?'

'I really don't know. I'm just flabbergasted. Or as Aunty Lil used to say—'

'Jiggered!' he said.

And at the same time I said, 'Jiggered!'

We laughed.

'How about I make a suggestion? Would that be acceptable?' he asked.

'Please do. I really can't think straight right now.'

'How about I drive you round to the house now? You can see how you feel when you get there and if you feel like you want to stay, then that's fine, but if it doesn't feel like the right thing to do then I can take you to the hotel.'

Nodding, I thought of how kind it was for him

to offer. But then I realised he must be too busy for this type of errand.

'I could get a taxi. I don't want to put you out.'

'Miss Wagstaff—'

'Nell, please call me Nell.'

'Thank you. Then in that case, Nell, I insist that you call me Dominic, or Dom. It would be my pleasure to do this. When Lilian and I last spoke a few weeks ago, she asked me to make this as easy for you as possible, when the time came, so I wiped all my appointments and I have a free diary this afternoon so that I can take you. It's what Lilian would have wanted. But only if you want me to. I don't want to impose.'

'It really is kind of you and I appreciate it very much. Yes please. I would like you to take me, Mr... erm... Dominic.' My hands were shaking and I wasn't sure how I'd even get to the house alone in my state.

'Let me take your case, and we'll go down to the car park. The house is just a two-minute drive away.'

Dominic stopped and pointed his key fob at a smart black Jaguar saloon. He popped my case into the boot and opened the door for me. He really was very kind. I looked over at him while he was driving. He was quite handsome in a geeky type of way. He had blond hair, which looked like it needed a cut, but strong cheekbones and his glasses sat on quite a large nose, but it suited his face perfectly. I had no idea how old he might be, maybe mid-to-late thirties. I had to stop myself from staring. He could be married with four children for all I knew about him.

My heart was racing as we approached Larkspur Lane and glided to a stop outside of number 37. I gasped. It was exactly as I remembered it. How, after all these years, could it look the same? I couldn't move from the car, I needed to breathe it all in.

The front garden was as immaculately maintained as ever. Behind the wrought-iron railings and gate, two glorious hydrangea bushes stood proudly either side of a stone path, with bedding plants all the way along, that led to the house. It showed no signs of neglect by being owned by an old lady.

I had always adored this house. The identical big bay windows either side of the double wooden front doors were perfectly symmetrical. Above the front door, set back quite a way, was an impressive stained-glass, arched window, flanked by beautiful French doors, which I knew belonged to the two front bedrooms. They opened onto that stunning veranda balcony, the thing I remembered most, which stretched across the front of the house with wrought-iron railings all around to match the garden fence. The house was still as stunning as I remembered.

Since receiving the letter, my memories of the house and the time I spent here had been gradually coming back, more every day. I glanced at the house to the right, remembering Jack Shepherd. The first boy I ever had a crush on. He was the boy who gave me butterflies deep inside my tummy. The boy I shared my innermost thoughts with. I loved him deeply but he never knew. No-one did. It was my secret.

We spent many summers on the beach just over the road, collecting shells, crabbing at the quay down the road and sometimes just chatting about life and how our lives would turn out. His love of animals sprang to mind just then and I smiled. It had helped to have a friend while I was here for those summers. He was the only one I told that my parents were having difficulties. I was fourteen the last time I saw him.

I wondered what sort of man Jack had grown into, and how his life had turned out. I'd probably never know. He and his family had probably long gone from here.

'Ready?'

Lost in my memories I had forgotten that Dominic was sat beside me and his voice startled me.

I gave a little shiver, looked at him, then up at the house once more, and after taking a huge deep breath, nodded.

'Yep. Let's go.'

He let me lead the way. Either side of the gate which led up the garden path, someone had painted on some large rocks. On the left side the word on the rock was *Welcome*. On the right side it said *Home*. They were so pretty and it felt as if they'd been placed there just for me, although when I thought about it logically, they could have been there a while. I'd read a lot this year about people painting rocks for others to find to try to cheer them up. I smiled as I walked up the garden path and put the key in the front door's lock. I hesitated before pushing the door open and entering the large square hallway. The first thing that hit me was the smell. It smelt just like Aunty Lil. It was a mixture of Lily of the Valley perfume and talcum powder and it took my breath away. I half expected her to come out of the kitchen to welcome me with open arms, just like she always had.

The next thing I noticed was how quiet it was.

Aunty Lil always had the radio on. She used to sing and dance around the house all the time. She was such good fun to be with and had said that music and dancing lifted the spirits. When I was sad, she'd drag me up to dance and – she was right – it had made me smile every time. I grinned now at the thought of her swinging me around in the huge hallway.

I was aware of Dominic's presence behind me, and found it reassuring. I knew that Aunty Lil had passed away in the house, and though I wasn't sure whether I wanted to know where, I knew that if I didn't ask, I would always wonder.

I turned quickly and collided with Dominic's chest. Woah! I wasn't expecting it to be that firm. What was he hiding under that dishevelled appearance?

'Shit! Sorry!' I laughed.

'Erm, oops, I'm so sorry,' he muttered as he went bright red and fumbled around in his top pocket as he stepped back and pushed his glasses back up his nose. He brought out a packet of mints as if he'd been looking for them intentionally.

I shook my head as he offered me one.

'Dominic. Where did she…?'

He bit his lip, and I think he was wondering whether to tell me the truth.

'She was in the lounge, in her favourite chair, looking out of the front window.'

I smiled. She'd loved the view from that window and I didn't blame her.

Walking through the door on the left, I entered that very lounge. I walked over to the winged back armchair. It would have been at least thirty years old, as she'd had it ever since I'd been coming here. A gasp escaped my lips. The sun sparkled off the turquoise-blue water of the bay, lapping the soft white sand. I rested my hand on the back of her chair and knew that she would have loved that view being the last thing she ever saw.

I wandered from room to room downstairs, breathing in the familiarity of this beautiful old house. The rooms flowed perfectly, each a continuation of the other; a sunroom, which I'd always loved, overlooked that pristine garden at the back of the house and led into the large kitchen, which in turn led into the dining room and then back into the hall. It hadn't changed much over the years apart from being modernised and it felt as if I'd never been away. Being here felt completely right. It felt like coming home.

However, I also felt so sad that she wasn't here with me. And I regretted that we'd missed out on spending time together over the last twenty years or so. Whatever had been said between her and Mum must have been very serious for it to have created such a rift. I wondered if I'd ever find out the truth. I felt guilt, too. Guilt because I never did anything to try to get in touch with her.

Once back in the hall, I felt the pull of upstairs. The staircase was directly in the middle of the hall and split halfway up, to ascend either way. At the top was the large bathroom, with a bedroom towards the right. To the left was the library cum spare room, in which I used to stay when I visited, and Aunty Lil's bedroom. I meandered into the library. It still looked exactly the same – dark wood shelves filled with classic novels. I turned my head sideways to read the titles and I wasn't surprised to see that Dickens still sat amongst the Bronte sisters, and that the left-hand side was filled with many volumes of the Encyclopaedia Britannica. She'd collected them in a subscription and she used to wait until I visited so we could put them together, sitting side by side, listening to old records on the radio. Such happy memories.

Dominic's nervous cough brought me back to the here and now.

'Do you have any thoughts about what you'll do with the property, Nell?'

'I have no flipping idea, Dominic. Two hours

ago I'd never owned a property in my life. I could only ever afford to rent. And now I have this.'

'And a beach hut don't forget. And a substantial amount of money.'

'Oh don't! It makes my head hurt.'

'I can only imagine. And please do call me Dom. Only my mother calls me Dominic.'

We grinned at each other. He really did have a lovely, kind face. I liked him.

'Well, how about we take things one step at a time? Maybe for right now all you need to think about is whether you'd like to stay here tonight, or whether you'd like to stay in the hotel. We should probably let them know soonish.'

'I don't think there's really a choice. I want to be here. I can feel Aunty Lil here all around me, and I don't think I could be anywhere else. This is where I feel I belong.'

'OK, let me message Sally and get her to cancel, if you are absolutely sure. And I'll make sure that she's transferred the money into your account now we have the details.'

'I am and thank you. Thank you for everything so far, Dom. You've been brilliant and I don't know what I'd have done without your support.'

'My pleasure, Nell. It's what Lilian would have wanted me to do. She'd have told me off had I not brought you here today. She knew what it would mean to you and wouldn't have wanted you to be alone. Oh and don't forget, the car is in the garage too.'

I tittered at the thought of me driving around in a little-old-lady car and thought that Aunty Lil would be laughing at me from above.

'Great, let's go take a look.'

Chapter Eight

T O GET TO the garage, you had to walk through the back garden, and as we headed that way I noticed just outside the back gate that there was another painted stone. Perhaps Aunty Lil had painted them. This one was pink and green and the word *hope* was written in sparkly silver.

All the keys I'd been given were labelled, so I pulled out the one that said 'garage' and unlocked the door. I leaned down and pulled the garage door up and had the biggest shock of the day when I saw a silver Mercedes badge glinting in the sunlight. I looked around at Dom, who had the biggest grin on his face.

'Lilian was no little old lady you know. She was such a character. I told you she never wanted for anything. I take it you can drive?'

'Absolutely, I just couldn't afford a car on the wages I earned before I lost my job.'

'Oh I'm so sorry to hear that you lost your job, Nell. That must have been a shock.'

'My job and my fiancé in the same week. Careless, eh?'

He looked at me, with his head tilted to one side, as if he was about to say something, but then he looked away again.

'Well this seems very serendipitous in that case,' he said.

'Doesn't it just. Tell me I'm not dreaming.'

'I promise you are not dreaming, Nell.' He swept his arms around him. 'This is all yours.'

'It's just incredible. I can't take it all in.'

'Why don't we walk over to the beach, have a look at the beach hut and we could grab a coffee at the little café on the front. We can have a chat through some of the possibilities. I have a change of clothes in the car, would you mind awfully if I used the downstairs bathroom to get changed? I'd feel a bit daft in my suit walking on the beach.'

'Of course, be my guest.' I giggled. This was my house now after all. 'A walk on the beach would be delightful.'

Dom grabbed a small rucksack from his boot, and brought my case in too. I was so grateful to him for his kindness and his help. What a nice man he was. I stood at the front window and looked at the view beyond. It really was quite spectacular and took my breath away every time I looked at it.

'Shall we go?'

The sound of his voice, jolted me from my thoughts. I was daydreaming again. In jeans and an open-necked shirt, along with a pair of trainers, he looked ten years younger. And pretty hot too, I couldn't help but notice. I couldn't wait to text Shivani and tell her everything that had happened so far today. She'd never believe me.

Locking the door behind me and glancing up once more at Aunty Lil's house, or should I say *my* house, I shook my head.

Dom laughed. 'It's been a big day for you, Nell.'

'You can say that again.'

'I said, it's been a big day for you, Nell.'

We grinned inanely at each other and held the other's gaze.

Just opposite the house, there were ten or so steps, which took you down onto the golden sandy beach and then to the sea. It was shallow, if I remembered correctly. It was one of those beaches where the sea was quite close, not like some resorts where you had to walk miles out to paddle. It was the perfect beach.

We reached the bottom of the steps. To our left was the promenade which hosted rows of pastel-coloured beach huts. And to our right, a bustling café.

'Which first?'

'Beach hut I think, then coffee.'

'Excellent choice, Nell. Excellent choice.'

The more time I spent with Dom the more I liked him. When we first spoke on the phone he'd seemed stuffy and formal. But he was like an onion, with many layers. He had a good sense of humour and when he smiled his whole face came alive and his eyes sparkled the most beautiful bright blue.

We walked down the promenade and he stopped outside a pale-blue-painted beach hut, which had blue, green and pink flowery bunting across the eaves. On one door was the number 136 and on the other a plaque which said, 'Life is better in flip-flops'. I reached for the other set of keys from my handbag, the one with a small porcelain beach hut key ring. No way I could get these keys muddled up. Aunt Lil had thought of everything.

As I looked down, I saw a huge rock either side of the door. They had been painted in pretty pastel colours and then varnished. On the left one, it said *Beach Hut* along with an image of a colourful little hut. On the right one, it said *Life is what you make it* and there was picture of a house very similar to Aunty Lil's. Perhaps she'd been into painting in her later years. They were so pretty and I loved the words. They seemed like just what I needed now I was here in Muddleford. I felt as if I *had* come home and that Aunty Lil's messages could apply to me right now.

'May I?' Dom took the keys from me and moved forward to unlock the doors. 'Stand back, Nell.'

What lay behind, took my breath away. It was the prettiest little room I had ever seen. White-washed walls were adorned with more of the colourful bunting; two pale-blue tub chairs with matching footstools were perched at the front on each side; pastel blue, green and pink cushions were scattered around; and there was a crocheted blanket over the back of each chair. There was a large whitewashed wooden sideboard at the back, with a kettle and tea-making facilities and a small tabletop fridge. The floorboards had also been whitewashed and the space had that same Lily of the Valley fragrance about it as the house. This was unmistakably Aunty Lil's and I felt privileged to be here. But it wasn't hers any more. It was mine. I wondered why she'd had this as well as the house, which was just over the road. But then again, I supposed, if you could, then why not?

'Turn around,' Dom whispered, bringing me

back to the present.

The view out to sea was spectacular. A lone sailboat in the distance the only thing interrupting the horizon. The sun shone high in the sky and beyond the golden sand, and it created a picture-perfect image of a sea that seemed to shimmer with diamantes. It was purely stunning and left me stuck for words.

'If you did want to sell it, they are selling for between two hundred to two hundred and fifty thousand pounds. We had it valued quite recently.'

'You are having a laugh, aren't you?' I turned to face Dom.

'I'm extremely serious. I never joke about money. I'm a solicitor.' He winked. 'Come on, let's grab a coffee and I'll talk you through some more details about the valuations we've had done on the house, the car and the beach hut.' He really had thought of everything.

A sharp trill ring tone cut through my thoughts and Dom answered his phone, walking away from me slightly. In a low voice, I heard him say, 'I can't talk right now, I'm with a client. Yes, Lilian's niece. Yes, it's all going well.'

My thoughts drifted off as he talked and I studied him while I knew he had his back to me. He had an amazing body, a firm bum that fitted his jeans well, and broad shoulders. Now he wasn't wearing his suit, you could see that he was the type of person who spent time in a gym. I honed in on his last few words as he turned, and I quickly swivelled back round, hoping he'd think I'd been looking at the sea all along.

'Love you too. Bye, Tom.'

There went my fantasy of the fit solicitor and I having a more interesting relationship.

'Nell, I'm so sorry for that interruption. My husband likes to keep in touch with me during the day.'

'Please don't apologise. Come on, I'm gagging for a coffee and I want to hear all about Tom.' While I'd known all along, that we'd never be more than friends, after all, I'd only just come out of a relationship, I thought how nice it would be to have a friend in Muddleford while I worked out what to do before heading back home. I felt a huge sense of responsibility to do the right thing and try to work out what Aunty Lil would really want me to do with the inheritance.

We meandered towards the little beach café. Time seemed to have slowed down since I'd arrived here; the hustle and bustle of home truly behind me. I felt calm and at peace. I put it down to the sea air. The sea has always calmed me. When Mum and Dad used to argue when we were at Aunty Lil's I used to slip out the kitchen door and come to the beach, which is where Jack would normally find me. Just sitting looking at the sea. Sometimes I feel like my body is a battery and being by the sea refills my soul with joy.

Dom asked me whether I'd like to sit outside or inside. I chose outside. I'm much more of an outside person, especially when I get to the seaside. I hated to be shut away when I could be out in the fresh air.

He asked me what I would like and made his way over to the counter, so I grabbed my phone. Twelve missed calls and three messages from Shivani asking me where I am and how it's going. I dropped her a quick text.

Will message you later but all OK and oh boy do I have some stuff to tell you xx

I threw my phone back in my bag as Dom returned.

'I know you haven't had much time to think, Nell, but do you have any gut feelings about what you'll do with the properties? There are lots of options. You could sell. I have the valuation details of the house as well as the beach hut. The house was valued at £750,000.'

I gulped. How could a house even be worth that? That's three quarters of a million pounds.

Crikey, if you added the value of everything Aunty Lil had left me, I suppose you could call me a millionaire. How could it be that one day, I was scratting around to get enough money to pay for my bus fare and a meal deal from Marks and Sparks, and a week later I had everything. I just couldn't take it all in.

'It's weird, Dom. I've never owned a property and now, all of a sudden, I do. But it's not where I live or where my friends are. I suppose staying here is an option but a very remote one because everyone and everything I know is back home in Staffordshire.'

'But you'd already said that you hadn't got your job any longer and that your relationship is no longer, so maybe you could stay here a while, and see how you feel about it.'

This was very true. The only person who I really had back home, now that Callum and I were no longer together, was Shivani. I needed her to come down and help me to make a decision. She'd be rational and talk some sense into me. I'd ask her when I spoke to her later.

'Well, I suppose it's not like I have anything to get back for,' I said.

'Whatever you decide, one of the first things you'll have to do is to transfer all the bills for the house into your name. I have a list in the file of everything. You have all the time in the world to make a decision on the house. There's no rush.

'If you need any help to talk through any choices or decisions, I'd be really happy to help you, Nell. I know Lilian would have liked to know that you were in safe hands. There is one other thing we need to arrange… and that's the funeral. Lilian is with the local funeral directors in the town and they know that we were waiting for you to come down. They have left it as long as they possibly could but have booked in a provisional date but we can talk about that tomorrow. We don't need to decide right now. I can help you with everything though. You're not alone.'

'Thank you, that really does mean the world to me. I don't know how I would have done any of this without you'.

I looked out to sea. It continued to sparkle and I enjoyed the warmth of the late-afternoon sun. Aunty Lil always used to say that down here had its own little micro-climate and that the weather was always beautiful. I sighed. It really was stunning here. Maybe after a couple of weeks, I'd be bored of seeing the sea every day. What's that saying? Be careful what you wish for, because one day, your wish might just come true.

Chapter Nine

HAMMERING ON THE front door woke me the next morning. My heart was pounding. I had been hoping that after my early start the day before I might get a lie in. Bleary-eyed, I grabbed my dressing gown from where I had flung it over the top of my case the night before and walked to the front door while tying the cord around my waist. As I passed the mirror on the landing, I smoothed my hair down. Whoever was at the front door, didn't deserve to see my wild locks.

There it was again. Bang. Bang. Bang.

'Alright! For God's sake, stop the banging. I'm coming!' I grumbled under my breath. I looked at my watch and was surprised to see that it was actually 8.30 a.m. I'm normally a 6 a.m. wake up girl so perhaps my big day yesterday had all been too much. I had felt exhausted when my head hit the pillow last night.

I flung open the front doors wondering who the hell was there at this time in the morning. Imagine my complete and utter shock and amazement, when I looked into the face of someone I had once known, so *very* well, nearly twenty years ago.

'Oh my God! Jack Shepherd! Oh my God, is it really you?'

Despite me asking that question, it was unmistakably him. I would recognise those beautiful eyes and that floppy hair anywhere. The years melted away. How many surprises was I going to experience in Dorset?

I was greeted by his oh-so familiar grin and my heart did a little skip. I reached up to touch my hair and realised that this was the first time he would ever have seen me in my nightclothes as an adult woman, even though he'd seen me in them plenty of times as a child – we'd had pyjama parties together since we were toddlers. I pulled my dressing gown around me even tighter to cover my skimpy shorts and vest top.

'Good to see you, Nellie-bum! I've brought you breakfast.' He handed over a brown paper bag and I could smell the aroma of fresh baking. 'Hope you still like croissants for breakfast.' He spoke as if I'd only seen him the day before and not as if it was twenty years before.

The last time we'd seen each other was probably one of the most romantic and memorable moments of my life. It was all flooding back now and my neck and face began to get very warm and I was pretty sure it would be blotchy too.

'Nell!' He raised his voice. 'Back in the room, Nellie-bum. Still a day-dreamer then?'

I couldn't help but grin back at him. He had a one-thousand-kilowatt smile that made *you* smile back at him, no matter how you were feeling. It was something that I had loved about him as a boy. It hadn't mattered what type of mood I was in, the minute I saw Jack I was grinning like a loon.

'Jack! I can't believe it. Don't tell me you still live round here? How did you know I'd be here? How do you even remember what I like for breakfast?'

I had so many questions for this person stood before me. The last time I'd seen him he was a fourteen-year-old gangly, awkward boy, but one who gave me a fuzzy feeling in my tummy. It seemed he still did. That familiar skip of my heart when he was around, happened again. How could my body still do that after all these years? Perhaps it wasn't so mysterious. The man on the doorstep was six-foot of pure gorgeous beardy man. God he looked so good. And I did love a beardy man.

'Aren't you going to invite me in then?' he

grinned. 'The least you could do is make me coffee when I've brought your breakfast around.'

I was so glad that Dom had offered to drive me to the local supermarket before he dropped me back at the house last night so I could get some essentials in.

My heart thumped like mad as I stood back to let him in then followed him through into the kitchen. I turned away to fill the kettle, then flicked it on, trying to compose myself. It was unbelievable to see Jack, but he had moved to where I was and he was standing so close to me right now, I couldn't concentrate on the simplest of tasks. I moved towards the kitchen window, flapping my hands to create some air.

'It's warm in here this morning.' I excused myself and stretched up to open the window a little. It wasn't that warm at all but my body was on fire.

A wolf whistle made me turn to look at him again. His eyes lifted from my legs, travelled up my body and met mine.

'You've grown, Nellie-bum!' he winked. God, he really needed to stop doing that.

'And so have you, Jack. How on earth are you?'

'I'm great. Obviously it took a few years for me to get over the fact that you left me heartbroken when you abandoned me that night without ever getting in touch.' He looked deep into my soul as if questioning whether I remembered that night. 'But eventually I got over it, moved on and found new, even better best friends.' He smirked.

I couldn't help but stare at him drinking in every detail. I had loved that face so much back then, and had dreamt about it so many times over the years.

He smiled then to show he had been joking. It lit up the room and I couldn't help but grin back at, after initially wondering if he'd been really upset about what had happened. A little bit of me hoped that he had and that he hadn't moved on too quickly, that he had missed me a little.

'I'm so sorry about that. You know what my mum was like. She forbid me to have anything to do with anyone from down here. Even you. But surely you got the letter I wrote to you explaining everything I knew?'

'You wrote to me? I never got a letter. So you did think of me then? I thought that you may have been running away from something or someone, maybe even me, on that night.'

'I thought about you all the time, Jack. You were my best friend and... well... Mum found my first letter and ripped it up. Whatever had happened between her and Aunty Lil was so serious that she wouldn't allow me to have any contact with anyone from down here. I wrote again a few weeks later, and Mum promised she'd post it, but from what you are saying now I'd say she clearly didn't. I'd wondered why you'd not written back. I wonder now whether I'll ever find out what happened. With both of them gone.'

'I'm sorry to hear that you lost your mum, Nellie. That must have been so upsetting for you.'

'Thank you. It's been hard, I won't lie, but it's getting a little easier. It's been a good few years now, although sometimes it seems like yesterday.' I could feel a lump forming in my throat and knew I had to head off this feeling, like I always did before it overwhelmed me.

I laid the coffee pot, mugs and milk jug on a tray. I never did this anywhere else, but had always done this at Aunty Lil's, and it amazed me how very quickly I'd reverted to my old ways in this house.

'Come into the sunroom. I want to know all about your life. Where do you live now? What do you do? I want to know everything.'

I sat cross-legged on the sofa and Jack sat next to me. I'm sure he didn't have to sit so close, there were plenty of other seats in the room. His knee touched mine and an electric jolt ran through my body. My heart was beating so fast, I'm sure he must have been able to hear it from where he was sitting.

'Well to start with I don't live very far away at all.' He nodded to the house next door.

'You have got to be kidding me.'

'It's true. Sad, isn't it? Thirty-four years old and I still live with my parents. It works for us though. They had the garage converted years ago to a self-contained flat, which I live in. They're really looking forward to seeing you Nellie-bum, if you'd like to see them that is.'

I loved that he still used his childhood nickname for me. It made me warm and fuzzy, though it brought all my childhood feelings of unrequited first love tumbling back. I wondered if he'd ever known how I'd felt about him. I wondered what he would have made of that right now. I remembered that night again and could feel the heat rise up from my chest.

'Well, is that a yes?'

'I would absolutely love to. There's honestly nothing I would love more.' I hadn't realised just how much I had missed his family.

'Well, come for tea tonight. I've got to go to work for a few hours later, but hopefully not for too long, so I'll come and fetch you.'

'That would be amazing. Thank you. But how did you know I'd be here?'

'Dom rang me. I'm good mates with him. Have been since… Well, you know. He probably shouldn't have told me, really, because of client confidentiality, but he couldn't help himself because he knew what good friends we had been. I think he thought that you could maybe do with people you know, and who care about you, around you right now.'

'That was really kind of him.' The part of that sentence that I honed in on was the bit where he said that he cared about me. I thought that after so long he'd have forgotten all about me.

'Pass me your phone, Nellie-bum. I'll put my number in it, then you can call me and I'll have yours. Then if you get any issues while you are here, you can give me a yell.'

'Fab, thanks.' I fumbled to grab my phone from my dressing-gown pocket and it gaped open and exposed my left boob, which was barely contained in my vest top. I went bright red as I pulled the robe closer around me.

'Thanks for the flash!' Jack winked and I didn't know where to look.

My face was on fire.

'And you'll get to meet Norman tonight,' Jack said. 'You'll love him. I think you'll get on like a house on fire.'

I'd forgotten all about Norman. I was very much looking forward to meeting him though. He sounded like he was someone really special if he had brought love to Aunty Lil in her later years. I couldn't wait to meet him. It would also be nice not to be sat alone this evening with just my memories for company.

I thought back to last night when I sat in Aunty Lil's lounge – which I needed to remember was now *my* lounge – gazing out to sea at the amazing view of the glorious sunset, turning crimson red, burnt orange and vibrant gold until it disappeared over the beach, wondering what the future held for me. Right then, 37 Larkspur Lane seemed to be the most natural place in the world for me to be. I felt at home and at peace here. The familiarity of being here in Muddleford felt right.

Within such a short time of being here I felt a sense of belonging that I could honestly say I hadn't felt for a long time. Was it because I had so many happy memories here? Was it because there was a tiny bit of me that felt that Aunty Lil was still around me steering me in the right direction? I liked that thought particularly and definitely felt a sense of comfort from it. But what was I to do? I couldn't possibly stay here, could I? I had a life back in Staffordshire.

I had rung Shivani to talk things over with her. She was gobsmacked by the news and we'd talked on a Facetime call for over an hour. I'd taken her on a guided tour of the house and she'd said that she loved it and was coming down at the earliest opportunity. I was so looking forward to her visiting and showing her around all the old places I knew.

While she'd also lost her job when the company folded, she'd immediately joined her family business as their marketing manager which they'd been asking her to do for years. She was loving it so far, even though it was very early days and said that she wished she'd done it years ago, instead of being defiant and wanting to do something independently of those around her. But she had needed to find her own feet and was trying not to regret those years of working for someone else. We'd talked about the fact that everything was a lesson learnt to move you forward in life. Perhaps this inheritance was mine.

'Have you been anywhere yet?' Jack's voice brought me back to the present.

'Not really. I've been to Aunty Lil's beach hut

and the café on the beach. That brought back many memories,' I said. 'I can't wait to catch up.'

'What are you doing this afternoon?'

'I have no idea. I have to get the car insured at some point and get used to driving again. That was an incredible surprise, I can tell you, when I opened the garage door.'

He threw his head back and laughed. 'I bet it was. No little-old-lady car for Lil. Only the best Mercedes C-Class Cabriolet for her. She treated herself six months ago so it's nearly brand new and I bet it's got hardly any miles on the clock. She only ever used it to go to Waitrose. That's how it remained in that pristine condition without a scratch.'

I smiled at the thought of Aunty Lil driving around town in that very glamorous car and immediately felt pressure to keep it the same way. I'd never owned a car, even though I'd passed my test a few years before. I just couldn't afford it and there was always Callum's car, although he didn't really like me driving it.

'If you've got no other plans, will you let me take you out for a couple of hours before dinner tonight, Nellie-bum? I could pick you up at around three when I finish work. For old times' sake, hey?' He nudged my shoulder. 'Go on, Nell. Say yes.'

How could I possibly refuse?

Chapter Ten

ONCE JACK LEFT, I felt a little lost again, so I thought I'd make the most of the glorious sunshine and wander over to the beach for a walk. I grabbed the keys to the beach hut and threw a carton of milk and a jar of instant coffee in my bag. My trainers were at the front door, but as I went to slip my feet in, I was reminded of the sign on the beach-hut door and nipped upstairs to fetch my flip-flops from my case, deciding to see if life really was better in them.

The pace at the beach was slow, people meandered along as if they had all the time in the world. They seemed to be mainly either on holiday or retired, and every person who went past either smiled or said 'Good Morning.' What a pleasant change from the rat race at home, when people barely grunted at you as you walked to the bus stop.

I ambled along to the beach hut, copying the pace of everyone around me. When I reached number 136 I opened up the double doors and propped them open with the stones. Now I was on my own I could have a good mooch round. I didn't like to go rifling through everything in front of Dom yesterday. I found a small radio in a cupboard, which I took out and plugged in. I smiled as it tuned straight to Radio 2. I should have known Aunty Lil would have had some sort of music in there. It reminded me to hunt down a radio in the house too. It had been very quiet last night. There was a TV and a Freeview box, but I couldn't settle on anything properly. Perhaps it was because it was the first night in a different place. Plus I had a lot of things whirring around my mind about what to do with the house in Staffordshire, now I couldn't afford to live there alone, although now I actually could. My head hurt!

I noticed a microwave at the back of the hut, which I hadn't yesterday, and a door in the corner which I also hadn't seen. When I opened it, to my delight there was a tiny loo. Well, that was a bonus. All mod cons here. At least I wouldn't have to use the public loos, which in my memory had always had an extremely whiffy pong about them.

I filled the kettle with water from the sink and switched on the fridge. There were two deck chairs hanging on the walls, just inside the doors, and after a couple of attempts to put one of them outside the hut on the small area of raised decking just before the promenade, I sat down and drank my first beach-hut cup of coffee overlooking the sea, with the warmth of the sun on my body. It all felt oh-so good. I really did feel relaxed here.

Remembering that in my handbag there was a notebook and pen, I grabbed them and read what was already in my book. I loved a list. Nice stationery and a list. Sometimes it's the simple things in life that make you happy.

Page one of the book was headed up 'Wedding Cancellations'. There were still a lot of things that needed sorting but, right now, I had bigger things to think about. I turned the page, sucked the top of my pen and gazed out to sea for a few minutes, then I started to make some more notes which flowed onto the page without hesitation.

Choices to make:

1. *Live in Muddleford/Live in Staffordshire*

2. *Sell 37 Larkspur Lane/Rent out 37 Larkspur Lane*

   I needed to ask Dominic if he knew what rental price it would fetch. But what if I'd rented it out and then wanted to come down for the odd weekend?

3. *Short-term holiday lets/long-term rental*

Surely short-term would be harder work to manage/clean/keep on top of. I needed to do research into that.

4. *Sell the beach hut/Keep the beach hut*

If I did go back, I could come down for weekends if I fancied it but wouldn't have anywhere to stay. Could you sleep over-night in a beach but? Would I want to? More research needed.

5. *Sell the car/Keep the car*

I put a big tick next to 'keep the car'. I think I'd already made that nice easy decision.

6. *Look for a job/Do I want a job?/Do I need a job?*

Did I have an opportunity to completely re-think my career and think about what I'd love to do? I'd always loved reading and when I was at university did an English literature degree. Perhaps I could get a job proofreading. I could even think about setting up my own company. Or maybe I could see if there was some volunteer work going. The local library maybe.

This was all getting quite exciting and one question just led to another. Life was stressful back home. A constant treadmill. Not having a job to be constantly thinking about, or another person to be considering was actually quite liberating. I missed Callum, but the last few nights I hadn't missed the constant emotional worrying of whether everything was ok for him and whether the things I did were pleasing him. Then there were the practical things which were always left to me, like wondering what was in the fridge, or whether I needed to go shopping, the whole what to be cooking for dinner and what I could do him for his lunch to take to work the next day and not worrying about all the other day-to-day things that go on in my life in Staffordshire. I didn't actually miss Callum as much as I thought I would. I felt that it was more the routines and habits that we had formed over the years that I missed.

If I was going to be truthfully honest with myself, not having a wedding to plan and to be thinking of every five minutes, was a huge weight lifted from my shoulders. If I thought about it, the wedding had become something that was just a focus. I wasn't even sure that it was what I had still wanted as time had gone on. Callum's mum had had so much input into it, guiding us in how she wanted us to do things, I wondered whether it was what we had wanted at all – it was hard to say no to things while they were putting so much money into it. And while I'd been frantically saving to put some money towards the day to show that I could contribute, Callum had still been off shagging bloody Saskia and paying to stay away in hotels, so he clearly didn't care about the money side of things.

Right at the start, I had said that I'd have been perfectly happy to have gone to Barbados and got married on the beach. For me, not having family around to celebrate such a monumental occasion, meant that the one day that was supposed to be the perfect day of my life would be missing something vitally important, so there was always going to be a sadness around it whether it be in the UK or abroad. Over here, it was even more noticeable that I wouldn't have been on my father's arm, walking down the aisle to my intended. Callum's father had stepped forward and said that he would love to walk me down the aisle but, while it was really very kind of him, it really wasn't the same. But I couldn't say that without offending anyone so I went with the flow to make everyone else happy, even if I wasn't.

All of those thoughts had been clogging up my brain for so long, and now it was free I had room to explore new ideas. I'd never even thought before of setting up a business. I wondered if it was possible. I was sure Dom could help me with the legal side of things. He seemed like the fount of all knowledge and a general all round very good egg. And if I had to invest in the business and didn't start earning straight away, now that I had some funds behind me, I would have a bit of a cushion. While I knew money wasn't everything it really was going to be life-changing for me.

7. *Organise funeral*

This was a job I was really not looking forward to. I'd need Dom's help on this one. Or Jack's family. They would know who to invite. I didn't know who would want to come along. Maybe I could even talk to Norman about it later. If he'd been in Aunty Lil's life over recent years, then surely he'd know who her friends were and who I needed to ask.

8. *Organise wake*

Should I have it at the house or at a nearby café or pub? I suppose I couldn't decide until I talked to the others. Definitely something I would have to crack on with booking though.

I wished I had had the chance to talk to Aunty

Lil more over recent years and known about her daughter Sophia and shared some of her sadness. It would have been so much to bear on her own. She must have been so brave. I could kick myself for not making more of an effort to get in touch.

So often you can say that one day I'm going to do that, and yet you allow other things to get in the way. Before you know it, weeks have gone by, and then months. The next time you think about it a year has rolled past and then another. You really should make the time to do the things you want to do and say the things you really want to say. Time is something that you can never get back.

It was too late for me to make amends with Aunty Lil. We'd both missed out on the last twenty years. And that was downright silly. Because of a rift that had gone on between her and Mum, I'd lost one of the most important people in my life. And that stung. I could never make it right. *Why do people not make the effort?*

A lone tear rolled down my cheek. I missed Aunty Lil and the relationship that we had. Being back here was making me remember what a wonderful influence she'd been in my life. I'd never felt this emotional. Not even when Mum died, because there was so much anger inside me then.

People say that hindsight is a wonderful thing, but I think it's crap.

Chapter Eleven

LAUGHTER BROUGHT ME back to the present. A couple strolled past holding hands and obviously found something funny. I couldn't believe that I'd dozed off. Not into a proper deep sleep but one of those states where you knew things were going on around you. I could still hear the faint tinny sound of the radio in the background, but was too tired to keep my eyes open. It reminded me when, years ago, I used to ask my dad whether he was asleep and he would say he was just resting his eyes. I gave a sad smile. Being back here was evoking many memories and remembering that we were a happy family unit once upon a time. When Mum and Dad were great fun to be around.

But there were also many times when I had hated Mum and Dad being around me. When I used to lie in bed at night with my hands over my ears shutting out their yelling. They were the times that I used to crawl into bed with Aunty Lil and she'd put her strong arms around me and rock me to sleep. They were also the times when Jack and I would take off to the beach and sit under the old pier, and he'd let me cry and talk and get it all out of my system before I went home to be faced with it again. He had known my innermost fears and was my best friend in the whole world.

My tummy groaned. The DJ on the radio did a time check and I couldn't believe it was 2 o'clock. It was no wonder I was hungry. I'd had nothing since the morning when Jack brought the croissants round.

Jack. There it was again. I only had to think of him and my stomach flipped. It was so funny to think that I was still getting this feeling all these years later. I was sure it'd go after a day or two. Everything was new at that moment and I was going through so many emotions and feeling permanently discombobulated. I still couldn't believe that he lived next door.

As he was coming round at 3 p.m., I thought I'd better make a move back to the house. I hadn't been able to work out why Aunty Lil had the beach hut when she lived so close to the sea, but having a glorious cliff-top view from her lounge window wasn't the same as being right on the beach. Now I'd spent a morning there I totally got it. I felt as if my soul had replenished after only a few hours and my broken heart had started to heal a little bit. I knew I had a long way to go and that I was going to have to dig up a lot of old feelings and memories, and deal with them one way or another, but right then, I felt that I was getting there and like anything was possible.

Switching off everything, I locked the doors behind me and patted them.

'Goodbye, see you very soon,' I muttered.

I didn't want people around me to think I was bonkers talking to a building, but it felt like the right thing to do.

BACK AT THE house, I fought the urge to shout, 'Aunty Lil, I'm back,' like I always used to. There was a big difference in temperature between inside and out, and I shivered as I entered the hallway. I thought for a second that I saw a slight movement in the lounge, but when I went to investigate there was nothing there. It was just my imagination playing tricks on me.

Jack was going to be arriving shortly, so I ran upstairs and jumped in the shower. I grabbed a strappy flowery sundress from my case and teamed it with a cornflower-blue cardigan. I knew I should probably take some time to hang up my clothes in the wardrobe but I didn't really know how long I was staying. Was it really worth it? I slathered on some tinted moisturiser, which slightly covered up the pink glow from snoozing in the sun, slicked mascara on my lashes and a little natural-coloured lip gloss across my lips, and spritzed myself with Sarah Jessica Parker's Lovely perfume. Looking in the bedroom mirror, I fluffed up my hair.

The doorbell rang. Bang on 3 p.m. A little nervousness crept in. What on earth was the matter with me? I took a deep breath, and spoke to my reflection.

'Get a grip, Nell. It's just Jack.'

I ran down the stairs, flung open the front door and let him in. As he walked past me, I caught a waft of Hugo Boss. My body tingled. I'd bought some for Callum a couple of years ago but he hadn't liked it and it had sat unused in the bathroom cupboard. I had completely forgotten at the time why it smelt familiar, but right then a memory popped into my mind of buying some for Jack for his fourteenth birthday that last summer.

'At your service, m'lady.' He bowed then mock saluted.

I giggled. He'd always had the gift of making me laugh.

'Your carriage awaits.'

'Actually, I wondered if you'd mind if we went in Aunty Lil's car?' I said.

'Your car now, Nellie-bum. Of course! You can chauffeur me instead. Great idea.'

'I keep forgetting it's mine.' I grabbed the keys from the dish on the hall table and locked the front door behind us as we went out to the garage and opened it up.

I was glad at that point that the house had a double garage because the car seemed huge and I didn't fancy manoeuvring it out of somewhere smaller. I was so pleased that Jack was with me and confided that I was nervous about driving but knew I needed the practice. I took it slowly to start with, easing the car out onto the drive with a big exhale of breath. Jack talked about the day his dad had taken him and Aunty Lil to the garage to collect the car and he came back with her to make sure she was OK with everything.

'It's a warm sunny day, Nellie-bum. Get your top off.'

I swung round to face him and he grinned back at me.

'I think it's this button here.' He winked.

I went bright red. I seemed to be making a habit of this around him. Some things never change.

At the press of a button, I watched, fascinated, as the roof folded up and over before hiding itself in the boot. I pulled steadily out of the driveway and was told to turn right. After a short drive we arrived at the quay. Talk about memories. After driving around the car park a couple of times, trying to find a space that I liked, I parked right at the back, which was devoid of any other cars, managing to park in the middle of two spaces. Jack found it hilarious, but I explained that I'd never forgive myself if anything happened to the car after Aunty Lil had entrusted it to me.

As we reached the front of the car, he grabbed my hand and pulled me along to the far side of the quay, where there was a little kiosk that sold buckets and crabbing wire. After he'd handed over his cash, he filled the bucket with water from a nearby tap. All I could think of though was how perfectly my hand had fitted into his and how much my heart was fluttering. He went over and sat down right on the edge of the quay and patted the space beside him.

'Come on.'

Oh how we laughed in that next hour, first when he stood and toppled and nearly fell in, and then when I said I'd caught a massive crab which was pulling on the wire and it turned out to be an old shoe. I'd forgotten how it felt to laugh like I didn't have a care in the world. Jack was a good influence on me.

At one point he grinned and pulled me to my feet. We were millimetres from each other's faces. I held my breath. He reached towards me, his eyes looking from mine, to my lips, and I closed my eyes. I felt him kiss the top of my head most unexpectedly and whisper, 'Oh how I missed you' into my hair so quietly I wondered whether I'd imagined it. I could feel a flush creep across my face and neck. He saw my obvious discomfort and in that way he always used to, which he knew would get round me, smiled and yelled, 'Come on, let's go and get an ice cream.'

After passing on our crabbing gear to a young family who had been standing behind and watching us, their toddlers mesmerised, once more Jack grabbed my hand. It felt the most natural thing in the world and we ran across to the ice-cream kiosk laughing. I was totally out of breath when we got there.

'Mint choc chip still your favourite, Nellie-bum?'

I laughed. 'It is and you will probably order one scoop of chocolate and one of strawberry.'

'Actually you'll find I've changed since you

knew me all those years ago, Nellie Wagstaff.' He ordered from the man at the counter. 'Could I have one mint choc chip and,' he muttered under his breath, 'one with a mixture of chocolate and strawberry, please?'

He grinned and tilted his head in that very Jack way and my stomach fluttered again. I really did need to pull myself together. This was Jack. My friend. Just because I had a huge crush on him when I was younger, did not mean I had to behave like a schoolgirl every time he smiled at me now.

'Don't tell Mum that we've had pudding before we have dinner. She'll never forgive us,' he joked as we sat side by side on a bench. I was so aware of his firm thigh touching mine. 'I'm glad I finished work early now just for the ice cream. I suppose the company was alright too though.' He nudged my shoulder with his. There it was. That bolt of electricity. I wondered if he'd felt it too.

I let out the breath that I didn't realise I'd been holding.

'What do you do for work Jack?'

'I'm a vet. I went to uni and when I qualified it just so happened that another vet was moving on, so I got a job working in the local practice in the town. That's why I still live with the old 'uns, because I'm always at work and getting called out at ridiculous times of the day and night. Crazy really that I never moved far away. I only went to uni in Bournemouth and came home every weekend. But then, why would I want to leave all this?' He spread his arms around. 'It's the most beautiful place in England. And I get all my meals cooked for me, which really is a big bonus.'

'Oh wow. You always did say that you wanted to be a vet. How cool that you're living your dream.'

'Yes, it is I suppose. You have to make your dreams come true though, don't you? They're not going to happen unless you work hard and plan your future. Mum always laughs and says she doesn't know where my focus comes from. And what about you? What do you do? You always wanted to take on the world. Did you achieve your dreams too?'

'Sadly not. Well, certainly nothing as exciting as you. After we moved, I struggled at school and had to retake a year. Then I went on an intensive college course and worked my way up in various admin and secretarial jobs. I was promoted to an account executive in my last company but sadly they went bust recently, so right now I don't even have a job. What a loser, eh?'

'Well you could look at it like that, or you

could look at it a different way. That it's serendipity that has brought you here, that's brought us together again and that now you have inherited everything you have from Lilian, that you have an opportunity to take some time out, and work out what you do want to do. I'm a huge believer in everything happening for a reason but we don't always know what the reason is.

'You can rethink some new dreams and goals and, with Lilian's financial support, there is nothing to stop you achieving them. And if you need some help, your old pal Jack is still pretty good on the nagging front.' He patted my hand and I looked up into his beautiful blue eyes.

His hair had probably been loaded with gel earlier in the day but now it flopped forward in a haphazard way and he kept on sweeping it back. When he smiled, that childhood dimple still appeared in his left cheek. His short tidy beard looked so soft and it was all I could do to stop myself reaching out to stroke it.

He held my gaze for a little longer than was absolutely necessary and he looked down at my lips and then back up again at my eyes. God, I wish he'd stop doing that.

'This has been really nice, Nellie-bum. I've enjoyed spending time with you this afternoon.' He put his arm around my shoulders and gave me a gentle squeeze.

'Me too, Jack. Me too.'

'Lilian would love to have known she'd had an impact on your life even after all this time. She never stopped talking about you. You really should think long and hard about what you want to do with your life now. She'd be so pleased that she'd been able to help you.'

A lump formed in my throat and I could feel my eyes welling up.

'Come on, let's head back home, Mum will have the tea on and I can't wait for you to meet Norman. You are going to absolutely love him. He's quite a character.'

Chapter Twelve

W E'D HAD SUCH a lovely couple of hours and I felt completely relaxed and happy. I was so glad that Jack had been with me on my first drive out in the Merc. I felt a million dollars. A flash car *and* a gorgeous man in the passenger seat. It was great for my morale and I couldn't stop smiling.

We entered the Shepherd's house laughing loudly. Les and Val greeted us with open arms. It was so good to see them, and both looking so very well too. There were hearty hugs all round. Val always had been the best hugger I knew.

She pushed me to her arm's length.

'Let me look at you, Ellen Wagstaff! You're all grown up. I knew one day you'd grow into those lanky legs of yours.' I laughed nervously and she pulled me in for another squeeze. 'I always knew you'd turn out to be a beauty. Didn't I say that, Les? Didn't I?'

'You did, my dear, and of course she's grown

up. The last time you saw her she was only fourteen and that was twenty years ago.'

I smiled at Les and remembered what a kind man he had always been. If ever Aunty Lil needed a man's touch for something around the house, he was the first one she'd called and he would be there like a shot. If ever she was in trouble, in any way, Les and Val were right there for her. I was so glad that she'd lived out her years with them still as her friends and neighbours.

'I was so sorry to lose Lilian, darling. I'm so sorry for your loss, especially after everything else you've been through in your life. But I suppose we should be glad that her passing has brought you back to us. It feels so strange that she's no longer next door.' She reached a hand up to wipe away a stray tear. 'Just knowing that she was at home was always a comfort to us over the years; having a voice over the fence to shout good morning to. The nights I said to Les that I was popping round to borrow something and we sat and polished off a bottle of wine between us, and he'd come round two hours later to find us giggling on the swingy bench in the garden. We always managed to persuade him to join us and then we'd stagger home in the early hours. Good job we weren't far away! And obviously Norman was there too in later years. Such company for her. I'm so glad she found him.' Another tear rolled slowly down the side of her cheek and she took a tissue out of her apron pocket and wiped it away. 'Ignore me, I'm a silly old fool. Lilian wouldn't want me to be sad. I know that much. Come on, let's go through.'

Val tucked my arm in hers and covered it with her hand. She didn't seem to want to let me go and I was very happy for her to keep holding on to me.

Leading me through to the lounge, she put her hand over her mouth.

'A drink! How rude of me, I was just so happy to see you after all this time, and then I got chatting about Lilian, that I completely forget to offer you a drink. Can we get you a gin and tonic, or a glass of wine? What do you like to drink? It was dandelion and burdock the last time I saw you, but then you were fourteen.' She pinched my cheeks and giggled.

'A gin and tonic would be wonderful, if that's OK? It's not like I've got to drive home, is it?'

We all giggled and I sat on the sofa, but nearly flew off again when Jack flung himself down next to me and poked me in the ribs. He looked deep into my eyes and moved closer towards me. He coughed.

'Nellie-bum, I...'

'I'm *here*. Jack? Jack?'

A woman's sharp voice came from the hallway and Jack jumped away from me with a start. At the lounge door stood a tall lady with long black hair. She was pretty but I couldn't help but notice her heavy dark eyebrows and bright lipstick before anything else.

'Natalia, what are you doing here?'

Jack stood up and she wandered over to him, aiming for a kiss which seemed meant for his lips, but he turned his head away at the last minute, which didn't go unnoticed. She put her arm proprietorially around him while glaring across the room at me.

'Jack, darling. I saw your dad in the supermarket earlier and he invited me for dinner.' Her face changed and she plastered on a smile. 'And you must be... *Nell*.' She turned her nose up as she emphasised my name. 'It's *so* good to meet you finally.' She wandered over to me and I was taken aback as she air-kissed both cheeks. 'I've been hearing *so much* about you, especially in the past week.' Somehow she managed to drawl out that sentence to make it sound as if I'd been an inconvenience to her. 'It's been "Nellie this, Nellie that" every day.'

She grabbed Jack's hand and pulled him towards her, putting her hand on his back. He looked really uncomfortable and tried to pull away.

Val came in to wave us through to the dining room. 'Oh hello, Natalie, you're here then.' She winked at me.

'*Natalia*, silly, not Natalie.' A shrill giggle followed her words.

'Well you were christened Natalie, dear, so I'm not sure why you had to change it to something which sounds far too exotic for these parts.'

I'd never heard Val be bitchy before.

Jack took the seat at the head of the table opposite his dad at the other end, and Natalia nearly fell over her feet in her rush to sit as close to him as possible. Val put me in the chair the other side of him and opposite Natalia. I was sure she sneered at me when no-one was looking. For my part I couldn't stop staring at those eyebrows. They were likely to put me off my dinner and not much did that.

Val took the seat next to me and patted my hand. I noticed there were only five places set at the table and was a bit confused because I'd thought Norman would be here for dinner.

'Is Norman not joining us?' I asked.

Jack jumped up. 'I forgot about Norman. Bless

him! I'll go grab him.'

I was a little puzzled. What strange terminology to use about picking up an old man. I assumed that's what Jack had meant. He must live nearby. But why on earth wasn't the table laid with a place for him? Perhaps I'd been mistaken and he was joining us but not for food. Maybe he'd eaten earlier.

'So when are you going home, Nell?' asked Natalia, smiling sweetly.

'You never know, Nellie might be here to stay,' answered Val, smiling back across the table.

'Oh God, why would you want to do that? It's awful around here. Nothing to do at all.'

Val jumped in again. 'She hasn't made her mind up what she's going to do yet. Lots of options and no rush to make any decisions, is there my love?'

I had the feeling she was egging me on.

'Absolutely not. I might even stay here permanently,' I said.

Natalia physically balked at this suggestion and pursed her lips. 'I can't imagine why you'd want to do that. There's nothing for you around here. Surely you've got friends back wherever you've come from? The *Midlands* isn't it?' She made it sound like a dirty word. 'There are no job prospects. It's hard enough already to get a job if you're a local, let alone having people from elsewhere come in and try to take our jobs and other things that belong to us.'

I saw Val smirk before she got up and asked Les to help her bring the food through. I wasn't a horrible person and didn't want to fall out with anyone, so I tried to make conversation with Natalia while we were alone.

'Such a pretty name, "Natalia". Is it after someone famous?'

A compliment usually worked for most people but she just narrowed her eyes at me.

I tried a different tack. 'Do you live far away?'

There was silence again, combined with a bored look. I'd never been very good at keeping quiet when there was a gap in a conversation and usually felt like I had to fill it even when I knew I was flogging a dead horse. One last attempt and I wouldn't bother again.

'Do you work?

This seemed to be the thing that cracked her. It was as if a light switched on in her brain, and once she started chatting, she wouldn't stop.

'I do work, yes. I'm one of the senior staff at the vet's practice which Jack is a partner in.'

Partner, eh? He hadn't mentioned that when

we were chatting about his job.

'It's wonderful that we get to work together all day every day. Obviously when we marry and have children, that will all change, and I'll give up the job to raise our family.'

My heart sank to the bottom of my stomach. It seemed there were a lot of things Jack had forgotten to mention. I could have kicked myself for being so naïve, thinking he'd ever be interested in me, when he clearly had the beautiful Natalia around him all day long.

'Are you engaged then?' I asked.

'Well, not officially. But can you keep a secret, Nellie?' I had hardly finished nodding before she continued regardless. 'He asked me on the last Valentine's Day. He's so romantic, of course, but we're keeping it a secret for the moment. Please don't tell him I've told you, he'd kill me. He hasn't even told his parents yet. He wants to announce it when the time is right. That's why I'm not wearing a ring yet. Promise me, Nellie. Is it OK if I call you Nellie? That's what everyone else is calling you, and we're practically going to be family soon, aren't we? After all, you and Jack are like brother and sister, aren't you? That's what he told me, although you are prettier than I thought you'd be. Jack said you were a proper plain Jane and you're not that bad. Maybe one day I could take you to the beautician's and get your brows done. You can hardly see yours and thicker brows are all the rage now. Wouldn't that be fun? Oh and eyelashes too! A proper girl's day out.'

What a change of direction.

'Erm yes, I suppose so.'

I couldn't take my eyes off her face. She couldn't be older than I was, but she'd clearly had a lot of work done on her lips because they were absolutely massive and proper permanently pouty. I couldn't imagine how she could drink anything without dribbling it all down her chin. And she could get stuffed if she thought I was letting anyone near my eyebrows. Sluggy-eyebrows and spider-lashes were not a fashion statement that I wanted to be any part of.

Les and Val returned to the room laden with umpteen bowls of food. Val always had been a feeder.

'Everything all right?' Val asked nervously.

'Oh wonderful, Val, darling. We're getting on like a house on fire, aren't we, Nellie?' She smiled that sickly sweet smile again.

I really didn't know what to make of her. She had started acting like my best friend but I didn't feel comfortable around her at all. I felt like she was someone I needed to keep aware around and maybe not fully trust until she'd earned it.

'Here he is.' Jack interrupted the conversation when he returned to the room. 'Come on, Norman, come and meet Nellie-bum. Nellie-bum meet Norman.'

'Fuck! Oh my god! Shit, I'm sorry! I didn't mean to say fuck. But really! Oh, err hello there.'

Norman was not what I was expecting at all. In my head, I'd built a picture of a grey-haired, cravat-wearing, smooth-talking older gentleman who had won the heart of Aunty Lil. But the Norman who shuffled in behind Jack, couldn't have been further away from my imagination.

Chapter Thirteen

I LOOKED INTO Norman's big brown eyes as realisation hit me. Norman was in fact a curly haired, slightly scruffy-looking, white-blonde poodle.

'This is Norman. Are you serious?'

Jack reached down and tickled Norman behind the ears. The dog leaned into him in ecstasy.

'Yes, this is Norman.' He looked confused. 'What on earth did you expect Norman to be? A human?' He laughed out loud at how ridiculous that sounded and then looked at my dazed expression. 'Oh my God. You did.'

'Of course I did. Everyone was talking about Norman like he was a person. That he was the love of Aunty Lil's life.'

'He was. That's absolutely what he was. They were inseparable and when Lilian was found, he was sat curled up at her feet.'

'That's just too sad,' wailed Natalia from the other side of the room, finally realising that everyone's attention was elsewhere.

Jack rolled his eyes at me and ignored her. 'I grabbed all his stuff and brought him round here immediately. I didn't think he'd need all the upset of the doctor coming out and the funeral directors taking Lilian away.'

I flinched at the thought. That was not a picture I wanted in my mind.

'Sorry. Come and say hello, Nellie-bum. He's really gone into himself these last few days. Poor little soul doesn't know what's going on and he keeps going to the back gate and sitting waiting, don't you, mate? I'm sure he's waiting for Lilian. If she went out for a day, he'd come round here to stay and wait for her to come back.' His voice wavered as he continued to rub his ears. 'Get down to his level and just take it really easy to start with. He needs to get used to you, before he trusts you.'

Slowly, I lowered myself on the floor next to the dog and held my arm out to him. He cowered away from me and I looked up at Jack.

'It's OK, don't give up after once. Maybe just sit for a minute or two and see what he does. I'll grab his bed and he can lie in that while we eat dinner.'

Norman looked at me, and I smiled at him. Daft mare. Why was I smiling at a dog? But it seemed like the right thing to do. He got up and came over for a sniff but as I lifted my hand slowly to try to stroke him, he shied away again.

'It's OK, Nellie-bum, he just needs to get used to you. Let's have dinner and then when he's heard your voice for a while we can try again. Come on Norman, bed.'

Obediently, Norman trotted off to his big squishy bed at the side of Jack's chair and put his head on his paws. He looked so sad and every so often glanced up at me, those big brown eyes boring into my soul.

'Jack, I do think that now Nellie isn't fourteen any more you can probably drop the ridiculous nickname. Why on earth she'd want you calling her that now I shall never know.' Natalia drawled.

'I like calling her that. It takes me back twenty years to when we were young and wild.'

He winked at me and grinned and my heart flipped over. How did he do that?

Natalia rolled her eyes and then glared at me from across the table. She hated me, I could tell.

Dinner was delicious. Val had always been a fabulous cook and she'd made a chicken, ham and leek pie, with buttery mash and fresh vegetables. Natalia seemed to re-arrange the food on her plate rather than eat much of it, although perhaps she couldn't use a knife and fork that effectively, with her long pointed, painted talons. I wondered how she managed at work. I wouldn't have thought veterinary nurses were allowed to have long nails, but hey, what did I know?

Pudding was a cinnamon crusted rice pudding. Val grinned as she put the dish down on the table. 'Hope it's still your favourite, Nellie.'

'Oh Val! I'm drooling just thinking about it eating it. Thank you so much.'

'Well, I wanted to celebrate your return to Muddleford in style and what better way than my signature dish and some proper comfort food.'

Natalia pulled a face across the table at me. Jack spotted it and she immediately smiled at him and blew him a kiss.

Les stood up. He was a man of few words but when he did speak, he liked to make them count. 'I'd like to propose a toast. Grab your glasses folks.' We all did as we were told. 'I'd like to say how delightful it is to have Nellie back within the family again. Welcome home.'

Natalia looked at me through slitted eyes across the table. If looks could kill, I'd be dead.

Despite her ridiculous behaviour, I was loving being back with these wonderful people. Even if Jack was engaged to Natalia, I would still love him to be in my life as a friend. Being in his presence felt so good. Like the sea, he seemed to fill my soul with joy. All those childhood memories flooding back felt good; times when life was perfect and those when they weren't, being cocooned in a world where I was shielded. He was always my way out, my protector, and I had always loved spending time with him. And that hadn't changed. That afternoon had been so much fun.

Les continued. 'We hope that you'll stay, but if you don't, we understand.' I looked over at Jack who gave a sad little smile. 'And we hope that wherever you and Norman will be, you'll be very happy in your new partnership. Join me in raising your glasses to Nellie and Norman.'

Everyone raised their glasses. Everyone except Natalia that was.

I had already started taking a sip when the shock of what Les had said, made my drink go down completely the wrong way. I started to cough and couldn't get my breath, my face was turning puce but I did manage to blurt out, 'Nellie and Norman?'

Val came over and rubbed my back in gentle circles, calming me. 'You didn't tell her did you, Jack? You are an idiot boy.' She playfully cuffed him round the back of the head.

He grinned. 'Erm... I thought it would be a nice surprise tonight.'

'I think you'd better tell me what's going on here, Jack,' I said.

'Lilian left all her worldly possessions to you, Nellie-bum. Everything. Including Norman.'

'But I've never owned a dog in my life.'

A big tut came from across the table and when I looked up Natalia was picking at her nails and couldn't look more bored if she tried.

'It's hardly rocket science is it?' she said.

'How can I look after a dog? I can barely look after myself. I've just managed to lose my fiancé *and* my job. What if I lose Norman too?'

Tears streamed down my face as the emotions of the last few days caught up with me. I'm not a pretty crier like Cheryl Cole-Tweedy-Fernandez Versini or whatever she calls herself these days. She slowly releases little diamante tears from her tear ducts and they gently trickle down her cheeks until she wipes them away. When I cry, I can't catch my breath, I make hiccuppy-come-burpy noises and my tears gush out, which mingle with snot and manage to congeal on my chin, leaving behind mascara stained cheeks, bright-red eyes and me looking an absolute fright.

I bet Natalia didn't cry like me.

Jack stood and walked over to me and cupped my face in his hands. After wiping my cheeks free from tears with his thumbs, he wrapped me tightly in his arms and whispered into my hair, 'It's OK, I'm here. I'm here.' For a moment or two, I relaxed in his embrace and extended my arms around his back holding him tightly as if there was only the two of us in the room. This is exactly how he used to hold me all those years ago. When life was crap and he was the light in my darkest of days.

My brain kicked in and I remembered that, firstly, we were in a room full of people and, secondly, he wasn't actually mine and that I had no right to taking advantage of his kindness especially in front of his fiance. If I was her, I'd hate me too right now.

I pulled away and looked across at her. She was tapping her talons on the table and her nostrils were most definitely flaring. She wasn't a happy bunny, as I'd expected. If I wanted Jack in my life, as a friend, I needed to make an effort to be *her* friend. I would do that for Jack and the sake of us having a relationship at all.

'I'm sorry,' I mouthed over to her.

A quick forced smile came back from her, but it didn't reach anywhere near her eyes. Although that could have been because of Botox.

Norman seemed to be cowering in the corner even more, wondering what all the noise was about.

'We're all here to help you, Nellie,' Jack said. 'There's no rush. Why don't you try to sit near Norman's bed and see what happens.' I looked up at him and he nodded. 'You'll be fine.'

Wiping my eyes once more, a little embarrassed about my outburst, I sat on the floor next to Norman again. His big brown eyes looked back at me. He looked so sad. I held my hand out to him but he just kept looking at my face and then my hand, unsure of what he should do.

'Here, let me grab some treats. That might do the trick.'

Jack left the room. I could feel the heat from Natalia's eyes burning into my back.

When Jack returned, he gave me the bag of treats and told me to put one into Norman's bed to start with so he could take it without having to come near me. For about ten minutes, we gradually teased him with the treats with him getting nearer before retreating to his bed. We got our breakthrough when he got up and sat nearer to me. I placed the treat on the floor. Those big brown eyes looked at me for reassurance.

'Go on, take it.'

He took the treat and looked at me again.

'Want another one?' This time I placed it flat in my hand and held it out. There was that eye connection again. 'Go on, Norman, take it.'

He got up and slowly and edged closer and closer until he took the treat.

'Good boy!'

He wagged his little tail. We repeated this a few times and eventually he sat next to me.

'Take it easy, but see if he'll let you touch him. Just try and stroke him, but let him see where your hand is going so he doesn't get any surprises,' advised Jack.

Reaching out gently, I lowered my hand towards the side of his head, maintaining eye contact and smiling at him. In my head, I thought that if he realised I was smiling at him, he would know I wouldn't be trying to harm him. He leaned into my hand, only a slight movement, but it was definitely there. I breathed out.

'See, you can do it. I knew you could, Nellie-bum.'

Jack gave me a grin that had just the right amount of cute mixed with sexy as hell, so that as our eyes met, unexpected heat rushed through my body. I really felt I could be in a lot of trouble if I didn't sort myself out with these ridiculous feelings for another woman's man.

The noise of a chair scraping on the wooden floor broke us from our moment. 'Jack, darling, could you walk me out to the car, please? I need to go, but I need a private word with you.'

The magic was well and truly broken, as I'm sure Natalia had intended. Although if my boyfriend was openly flirting with someone in front of me, I'd be mighty pissed off too.

'Nellie. It's been...' She ran a hand through her hair, glancing between Jack and me and held my glance. 'Erm, interesting?' She raised her voice at the end to make her point. 'Let's do lunch, darling. Soon.'

This girl ran so hot and cold, I couldn't work her out. I didn't know if the niceness was for everyone else's benefit or whether only I could see through her to see the bitterness that she clearly felt towards me. She air-kissed us all as she swept out, leaving a cloud of heavy perfume behind her.

Val grabbed a can of air freshener and sprayed it around, winking at me.

The dining-room window overlooked the drive, and we could hear slightly raised voices and see that Natalia was waving her arms around and poking Jack in the chest. Oh dear. It looked like he might be in trouble.

Chapter Fourteen

NORMAN RAN TO the gate, whining with excitement and spinning round in circles, when he knew he was going back to Aunty Lil's house. It broke my heart when he sped in the house and ran from room to room, barking, presumably looking for her.

Eventually, all went quiet and when I went into the lounge he was curled up in a ball on Aunty Lil's chair. I wandered over to him and gave him a little rub behind the ear. He just rested his head on his paws woefully, those big brown eyes looking so sad.

I heard a noise behind me. Jack had helped carry over Norman's belongings and had followed me into the lounge after putting the dog's bed and bowls in the kitchen.

'Do you think he'll be OK, Jack? You hear of animals having a broken heart sometimes. Do you think we'll be OK together? Do you think I can even look after a dog?' I had so many questions and thoughts whirling round my head. 'I'm scared, Jack.'

It was so hard for me to admit something like this but if I shared it with anyone, I wanted it to be with Jack. I'd spent the last years since Mum had died protecting myself from being hurt. I had started to realise that maybe that was why I settled for Callum – because I thought he was a safe bet. How wrong I was. However, I had also started to realise that Callum wasn't the love of my life after all.

In recent years I only had to worry about myself, until Callum had come along and even when we moved into together, I'd been against having a pet. It felt like too much of a responsibility. I'd spent my later teenage years feeling responsible for Mum. I felt that it was my fault that she drank, that she got so drunk so she didn't know what she was doing or saying, how hurtful the things she used to say to me were. That her and Dad were OK until I came along and then everything changed between them.

I hated that everyone in my life seemed to leave me. Mum had said that Jack would have made the effort to stay in touch when he got my letter if he'd wanted to and I'd spent ages thinking that he wasn't interested and had been glad to see the back of me. But knowing what I know now, that Mum didn't post that letter, I hoped he had cared and he did think about me and us, and what we had.

Jack walked over to Norman, knelt down next to the chair and stroked his head.

'You'll be fine won't you, boy? He'll just be sad for a bit. But I reckon you'll soon be the best of pals, and you're going to be great together. I think you'll both help each other to heal your grief. Lots of love and cuddles and fun and attention should do the trick.' He looked me straight in the eye and held my gaze.

I wasn't sure right then if he was talking about me or Norman. There was a huge bit of me that hoped it wasn't the dog.

'I've put all his food and bedding in the kitchen. I believe he used to sleep in Lilian's room but I'm not sure where you want him to sleep. I'll leave that up to you. Will *you* be OK tonight? Do you want me to stay for a bit? Do you want me to spend the night?'

Oh lordy! Now there was a suggestion I couldn't think about too much. I could feel the heat rising up my chest and into my cheeks. Jack's eyes bore into mine and I was sure he could see right into my soul and knew exactly what I was thinking. I really hoped not, because what I was thinking was positively pornographic.

I gulped. 'Thanks but I'm sure I'll be OK. The sooner I get used to being on my own the better, I suppose. And, anyway, I'm not on my own am I? I have Norman now.'

'Well, I'm only next door if you need me. Call me any time. And I mean any time.'

His habit of looking at me for longer than was absolutely necessary got me well and truly flustered every single time. It was those eyes of his. They were truly beautiful and I really had forgotten what a deep blue they were. What was going on here? Why was he so clearly flirting with me, when he was with Natalia? Perhaps it was just his way. Maybe I was mistaking his attention for something that was entirely different and totally inappropriate for me to think about.

'Shall we go for a walk on the beach in the morning, Nellie-bum? Shall I come and call for you?'

'Now that does make me feel fourteen, when you say it like that.'

We both laughed and it broke the tension.

'That would be lovely unless you have plans with Natalia.'

'There is nothing more I'd like to do on a morning off work than spend it with you and

Norman. We could have breakfast at the café. What do you think? About ten suit you?'

'It sounds perfect. Looking forward to a full English already, although after eating your mum's dinner tonight, I didn't think I'd ever think of food again.'

'She was so excited about you coming for dinner. She knew exactly what she was going to cook as soon as she knew. She's always had a soft spot for you. You know that. She loves you to bits.'

'It's so good to see your parents, Jack. I didn't realise how much I'd missed them. Well, all of you really.'

'Are you saying you missed me too?' He moved closer to me, creating that nervous tension again.

My heart began pounding. I really did need to control myself when he was around. I had no right to feel this way about him. Perhaps it was my emotions getting the better of me; it had been quite a week with one thing or another. The one thing that surprised me was how much I wasn't missing Callum. I felt freer than I had for a while. I'd started to realise that he'd been continually criticising me for the last few months. Not being around him felt like a huge pressure had been released.

I looked at this man stood before me. The boy

who I had once loved so much, who was back in my life but was now a big beautiful man. I wondered if he'd ever known the strength of the feelings I'd had for him back then. I hoped not. It would be embarrassing, especially as he was now with someone. But I couldn't stop thinking of those times twenty years ago, before we left each other's lives for what I thought was forever.

'Maybe I missed you a little bit. OK? Now be off with you. Leave me and Norman to get better acquainted.'

'I see I have competition already!' He laughed as I shooed him out of the lounge and he shouted, 'Don't forget to lock up behind me!' It was nice to have someone who cared.

Flicking on the TV, I searched for something to watch but couldn't settle, so covered myself with a throw and read a book while music played in the background. The house felt happier when there was music on and I'd always preferred reading to TV. I kept peering across at Norman, who seemed perfectly fine but didn't appear to want to leave Aunty Lil's chair.

At 10.30 p.m., my eyes were drooping and I could hardly stay awake.

'Come on, mate, let's get you out in the garden.'

He peered at me from under his furry eyebrows. He sighed and jumped down and had a big stretch before following me out to the back garden. I felt rather ridiculous standing in the garden trying to whisper loudly, 'Come on, Norman, do a wee!'

I heard a giggle from the garden next door.

'Night, Nellie-bum. Night, Norman. Sweet dreams.'

'Night, Jack.'

SOFT WHINES WOKE me and, as I came to, it took me a while to work out where I was and what the noise was. I dragged myself out of bed and there on the landing was Norman, sitting impatiently outside Aunty Lil's bedroom door. He looked up at me, and I nodded before I opened the door wider to let him in. He jumped straight onto the bed and curled up. I opened the balcony doors to let in some fresh air and could immediately hear the seagulls which made me smile. What a lovely reminder that I was so close to the sea. I sat next to him and he let me stroke his head.

'I'm sorry she's gone too, pal. There was so much I should have said to her.'

Looking around the room, Aunty Lil was everywhere, from her dressing gown hanging on a hook on the back of the door, to her perfume and hairbrush on the dresser. I wandered over and picked up the scarf that was hanging over the back of the chaise-longue and held it to my nose, breathing her in. I hadn't smelt that smell for twenty years but it smelt oh-so familiar.

Oh Aunty Lil, I wish I'd had the chance to see you. Why oh why didn't I fight my mother and insist that I stay in touch? Why did I not think of getting in touch and not telling her? Would it really have been such a betrayal? Why was it always too late to do some of those very important things that you really should have done? The saying that life is too short was so true. I made a pact with myself to make my life matter and to do the things that I wanted to do, while I had the chance. Who knew what tomorrow would bring?

'Come on, Norman, let's go and put the kettle on.'

As we walked through the hall I noticed that the time on the grandfather clock was 8 a.m. I slept well here. Norman had to be bursting to go out. I let him out and made a cuppa and decided that I was going to drink it outside. One of my many wonderful memories of my visits was Aunty Lil and I having a cup of tea in the garden first thing in the morning. We'd sit and chat on the swingy bench, with a blanket over our knees and put the world to rights before the breakfast. On the weekends we'd have a bacon sandwich or bacon and eggs and I'd cut the fat up into tiny pieces and throw them out onto the lawn, and before I'd even got back in the kitchen the seagulls would swoop down as if they'd been lying in wait and had never been fed.

The air felt so different here. It certainly smelt different from the busy polluted town that I came from. My phone vibrated in my dressing-gown pocket. I was delighted to see Shivani's name flash up.

'Morning, gorgeous, how are you? How's that beautiful seaside life going?'

'Oh, Shivani, you have to come and stay as soon as you can. It's glorious. I feel relaxed and at peace with the world. The pace is so different to back home. When can you come?'

'Not for a while, I'm afraid. While it's lovely to have been made an aunty again, it means that my sister's absence in the company business is really felt and it's all down to me. Don't tell anyone I told you, but I'm absolutely loving working with everyone here. I wish I'd done it years ago.'

'I'm really happy for you, mate, but I do miss you.'

'I miss you too, sweets, but if you say it again I'll cry, so amuse me and tell me what you've been up to.'

A little yap prompted the next half hour's conversation. I told her all about our jaunt out yesterday afternoon and how I was the proud owner of Norman the poodle.

'Oh my God! He's not one of those ridiculous-looking poodles that get shaved in some places and just have weird-shaped bits everywhere else is he?'

'No, thank goodness he's not. His coat is quite long and curly so he's just a big fluff ball. I'll send you a pic. Anyway, I'm going to have to go soon because I'm going out for breakfast with Jack.'

'Are you going on a date, you dark horse? You've only just got there. You're a quick worker.'

I giggled and lowered my voice and hoped that there was no-one in their garden. 'No, don't be daft. Jack was my best friend from years ago and we're just getting re-acquainted.'

'Mmm, I bet you are, you old slapper! What's he like?'

I laughed at her turn of phrase. 'He's tall and rugged, I suppose you'd call him. Looks like he works out. He's got dark-blond hair that he wears gelled back and sometimes it flops over his big blue eyes. He's got dimples and a cheeky grin that makes you want to smile back at him. He's got a short tidy beard that's more fluffy than hard and he's kind of cute, I suppose. If you like that sort of thing. He's just Jack to me.'

'Well he might be just Jack to you but the way you described him makes him sound fecking lush. My ovaries are twanging! Perhaps I will come down sooner than I thought. I think I need to check him out.'

I giggled. 'Talking of which, I'd better go and get dressed before he turns up and I'm still sat here in my dressing gown. It's so good to talk to you, Shivani. And I'll say it quickly, but I do miss you. Speak soon. Love you.'

'Right back at you, kiddo.'

Chapter Fifteen

JACK KNOCKED ON the door just before ten. Surprisingly, Norman and I were ready. It was a gloriously sunny day, so I'd chosen a pair of cut-off denim shorts, a vest top and a cardy, which I knew I could tie around my waist if I got too hot. Talking of hot, Jack was wearing a pair of designer trainers with long navy shorts and a tight royal blue t-shirt which showed off his well-toned abs and brought out the blue of his eyes. Not that I was looking that closely. I wondered if there were women who took their pets to the vet just to see him. The thought made me smile.

'What are you thinking about, Nellie-bum?'

I shouted for Norman to come and put his lead on, unable to meet Jack's eyes. I made a note to self: stop perving at Jack. Norman came running up to him, wagging his tail and jumping up excitedly. I wondered if I'd ever get that reaction.

'How's he doing?' Jack asked.

'I think he's getting used to me. He's not overly

friendly, and I think he's still struggling to work out where Aunty Lil is. When I came out of the shower earlier, I couldn't find him anywhere obvious but he was lying on her bed.'

'Aw mate. It's a big change for you, isn't it?' Jack ruffled Norman's ears. 'He'll be fine in time, I'm sure of it. You two ready?'

We crossed the road to the beach and at the top of the steps was another of the painted stones. I'd not noticed it the day before when I was with Dom. This one was painted pale-blue and pink and just had the word 'belong' on it, again in silver lettering. I smiled as I headed down the steps. I must have been dazzled by the sea the day before and completely missed it. Aunty Lil had been very busy.

It was still relatively quiet in the village, despite the glorious weather, and the beach was pretty much deserted. Jack said that it would be OK to let Norman off the lead. It was strange that Norman was my dog yet Jack knew more about him than I did. He filled me in some more on Norman's likes and dislikes. I wondered if this was what it was like when you were a parent, and only had your children to talk about.

'We do a dog social evening over at the vet's every so often. The next one is the night after next.

It's more about the owners making friends than the dogs, to be honest, but it's a really nice event. You should come along. They do group walks sometimes too. It's all about socialising and educating. We talk about how to look after your dog and what to look out for when you are out and about. For example, if you see a dog on a lead, and yours isn't, you should always ask the other owner if they'd like you to put yours back on. Some dogs are a bit reactive to others, so it's only polite. It's all that sort of thing that we discuss. It's really useful and you might pick up some good tips.'

I smiled both at his enthusiasm and his desire to teach me how to be a good dog owner.

'Sorry, am I boring you?' he asked. 'I'm always talking about animals. I must be so dull.'

'It's clearly your passion Jack. Tell me more about the practice.'

He went into lots of detail about his business. It was so lovely to hear him talk with such pride. He clearly loved what he did and it seemed the perfect vocation for him. I could listen to him talk about it forever.

'Jack! Where's Norman?' I held my hand up as the sun was blinding me. My eyes darted to the shore line and back down the promenade. My voice became an octave higher. 'Jack, I can't see him anywhere.'

'Don't panic. I know exactly where he'll be.'

And just as he predicted, the little bundle of fluff was sitting right outside beach hut number 136.

'Oh Norman, you clever boy.' I tickled him behind his ears. He leaned into my hand. Was this progress?

'Let's come back later to the hut. Only if you want to, of course. I'm blooming starving. Shall we go and order breakfast?' asked Jack.

'What about Norman?'

'Oh don't worry about him. They love dogs in the café. And we can sit outside. He'll be fine. Come on, son.'

Norman trotted along happily at our side.

'OH MY GOD! I can't eat anything ever again.' I patted my tummy. 'I'm the fullest I've ever been in my life.'

'They do a mighty fine breakfast here, don't they? They don't call them belly busters for nothing. And what better place could you wish to eat it, overlooking that.' He swept his arm out to the view beyond. It really was stunning. The sea glittered under the sun's rays and you could hear the gentle sound of the sea lapping the shore and the squawking of seagulls as they swooped down on any morsel of food they could steal.

The beach still wasn't particularly busy, just a few families with toddlers in shorts and t-shirts, building sandcastles, and the odd person brave enough, or some might say daft enough, to dip their toes in the English Channel.

We'd chatted easily over breakfast, neither of us short of something to say. The years felt as if they had melted away and I felt so at ease in his company. He talked about his job and how he had eventually been made a partner in the practice. I thought it was a good opportunity to bring up Natalia.

'So, Natalia seems, erm, nice?'

'I don't think she was particularly friendly towards you, to be honest. She's got a heart of gold when you get to know her, but can have a harsh exterior. She's great with the customers at the practice, though, and she keeps them coming back for me, so we all tend to pander to her a little bit.'

I suspected she wasn't the only reason lots of customers made return visits. If I had a vet that looked like Jack *and* he was nice to my dog, I think I'd keep popping to the vet's for the slightest of reasons. If the vet wasn't Jack of course.

'So, you and she?' I asked.

'Well, she wants it to be far more than it is, but I don't really want to talk about her right now, Nellie-bum. We need to talk about you and your intentions. Have you had any time to think yet?'

'I've done nothing but think. It just keeps going round and round in my head. Normally at around 4 a.m, hence the bags under my eyes.'

'To be honest, I think you look even better than you did yesterday. Your cheeks are rosy, your eyes are sparkling and you have a glow about you. You look utterly beautiful.'

'Ah you big smoothie.' I batted his arm, even though my insides were a lot less calm than I was letting on.

I wondered if he really thought I was beautiful. I'd always thought I was quite plain, even though Shivani told me I had good bone structure. I was definitely very different to Natalia with all that make-up, false eyelashes and fake tan. God it must have taken her ages to go to bed at night. But that was obviously what Jack liked in a woman, even though he didn't want to talk about her. I just had to keep reminding myself that he was just being friendly with me and that Natalia was his girl-friend, even if he didn't seem to want to admit it for some reason. Perhaps he was hedging his bets. There were some men who did that. Perhaps he wasn't telling me the truth. Natalia was under the impression they were engaged. Even though we shared a history, I really didn't know Jack as a man. He might not be the person I wanted him to be. People change a lot over the years and if he was a partner in a practice, he surely had some drive and determination, maybe a little womanising too. Looking like he did, he must have had women fawning over him every day.

Perhaps, however, I would go along to the next dog socialising session that he mentioned. It wouldn't do any harm to make some local friends, even though I wasn't sure if I was going to stay or go back to the Midlands. It was always good to meet new people. I used to make a real effort to mix with people before I met Callum and became quite insular. I could go back to being more open.

'Earth to Nellie-bum. Did you hear what I said?'

'Oh gosh, I'm so sorry, I was in a little world of my own.'

He laughed. Callum used to hate it when I let my mind wander and would get really narked with me.

'I said, shall we have a walk around the quay? Then we could go back and have a cuppa in the beach hut. I've got no work today, do you have any plans at all?'

'Apart from thinking about my future, I suppose not. And I could really do with walking off that huge breakfast. Come on, Norman, are you ready?'

It amazed me how a dog could go from fast asleep to full-on excitable mode within just a few seconds. I wished I had that energy. Despite Jack saying that I looked glowing, and while the sea air and the pace of life suited me, I really did feel like I had the weight of the world on my shoulders and some huge decisions to make.

'Maybe it'll help to talk through everything. I'm a good listener.'

'I'm sure you are. It would help, actually, thank you.'

He grinned at me. My tummy flipped. I really needed to stop this happening.

Going over all the options I had gave me an instant headache. I hoped that walking and talking would help me to find some answers. And walking next to Jack would at least mean that I could avoid getting lost in those gorgeous eyes.

After hearing me out, Jack said, 'No wonder your mind is blown. If it counts, I would like to say that nothing would make me happier than if you were around permanently, Nellie-bum. It's been so great having you here these last few days, and erm... well... my days have been brighter since you've been in them.' He bumped shoulders with me and grinned. His face was definitely showing signs of flushing. 'Don't tell anyone I said that though. I'm a rufty-tufty rugby-playing vet. Don't want anyone thinking I'm a big softy now, do I?'

When he smiled at me, it made me smile. I loved that he could do that and I realised that since I'd been spending time with him I'd smiled way more than I ever did back home. Perhaps it was because I wasn't in a job I didn't love anymore and that I didn't have anyone depending on me. Well, apart from Norman, of course, who was merrily trotting ahead of us on the promenade. Or perhaps it was because Jack still had the ability to make my heart flutter and give me butterflies in my belly, and that despite telling myself I had to control my feelings, I adored spending time in his company.

I knew it was wrong because of his relationship with Natalia, and for that it felt bittersweet, but I couldn't help myself. I didn't know whether it was because we had so much history and that at a time that I was experiencing grief, it was raking it all up again, or whether this was something new and there really was something between us. All I knew was that it felt as if there was a magnetic pull between us. And I was pretty sure I could do absolutely nothing about it.

Chapter Sixteen

SHAMEFULLY, FOR THE rest of the day, I did manage to put Natalia to the back of my mind. After stopping off at the beach hut, where Norman had a snooze and Jack and I had coffee after coffee and talked some more, we walked for miles and miles. Before I knew it, Jack suggested he walk me home in the early evening. Val had waved at me from her lounge window as we walked past their house.

A shiver had run down my spine as his lips gently brushed my cheek and as he'd walked away I'd touched the spot where heat radiated from my face. As a young girl, I'd longed for him to do that so many times. There had been a few heated moments when I thought he might kiss me, but it hadn't led to much until that last night. We were both young and I didn't know if he knew how I felt. I didn't know if he would even want to know how I felt and I certainly didn't want to do anything to jeopardise our relationship. It was safest just being the best mates that we could possibly be.

We'd talked a lot about what had happened after I left Muddleford, although that last night was never mentioned. I wondered if he'd even remembered that it happened. He'd had no idea of what Mum and I had gone through and I'd hoped that sharing some of it with him would make him realise that I hadn't abandoned him like he'd thought I had. That I'd had no choice.

Raking up those memories stirred up lots of emotion within me and as I sat in the garden room in Aunty Lil's house, looking over the back garden in the evening light, more recollections came flooding back.

When Mum and I left Muddleford firmly behind us, I grieved for months. Not only had we moved from our home and Dad had moved on in his life, but we also broke contact with Aunty Lil and everything we knew in the part of the world that had become my sanctuary while Mum and Dad were going through their incredibly rocky patch.

I had adored spending time with Aunty Lil, who had loved me so much. She'd made me feel safe, secure, loved and wanted and that helped me shut out all my troubles. Sharing my worries with

Jack back in those days, had also made me feel those things and had been incredibly helpful. He had really listened to me and when I'd needed to escape from all the anger and bitterness between my parents, he'd been there for me. When I'd sobbed, unsure of what life ahead was going to look like, he'd held me in his arms and comforted me, stroked my hair and told me that whatever happened I'd be OK, that he would make sure of it. He had been my rock. The best friend I had ever had. So when Mum moved us away from that wonderful environment which had been my escape from all the crap, I was totally devastated.

It was so hard but I really had tried to make an effort, throwing myself into my new school, joining every club I could in an attempt to make new friends. I'd spent so long lying to Mum about how I loved it there, to make her feel better, that when she got a call from the school to say that I'd hit someone, she was totally astounded.

'We do not accept violence in our school under any circumstances, Mrs Wagstaff, and Ellen will be suspended for two weeks.' I'll never forget those words or the shame on Mum's face. The headteacher, Mrs Wharton (or Mrs Wharthog as she was known), was a harsh woman, and I remembered wondering why she had ever become a teacher, because she belittled her pupils and criticised them at every opportunity. I also remembered, all those years later, how I couldn't help but stare at the massive mole above her eyebrow and wonder why she hadn't plucked out the huge dark hair that was sprouting from it.

I had tried to fight my corner back then. To tell her that the girl I'd hit and her friends had been constantly following me around, jeering at me and goading me with their vile, hurtful words. It wasn't just me they did it with either. And that particular day, I'd had enough. I had done my best to be a model pupil, my grades were reasonable, but those girls just didn't stop having a pop at me at every opportunity. And on that day, I took it no more. I lashed out. It had looked worse than it had been because when I smacked her in the mouth, the ring I wore on my little finger cut her lip. The ring Jack had given me the night before I left. Our friendship ring.

I'd tried to tell Mrs Wharton that the girl I'd hit, Denise Watson (I'd never forgotten her name), bullied not only me but others too, but she was having none of it. Mum discovered later that Denise's mum was the chairman of the parents and teachers association and Denise couldn't put a step wrong. It was totally unfair.

All the way home, Mum couldn't bring herself to speak to me. She'd slammed the front door behind her, and I could see the veins in the side of her head, pulsating.

'How dare you embarrass me in this way when I'm slaving every day to make a new life for us,' she'd yelled. 'Every day I have to go into that hairdresser's and listen to all those school mothers tell me how wonderful their daughters are and how many A+ grades they get and what model pupils they are. And then you do this. How could you do this to me, Ellen?' I always knew I was in serious trouble when she used my real name.

All the rage had seemed to bubble up and then deflate from her body as she'd flopped onto the bottom stair and held her head in her hands. I was aware that she was making it all about her and that she didn't really want to listen to what had been happening. I knew that there was a lot of pressure on her since we'd moved, but I felt like no-one was listening to *me* and how *I* felt.

'I'm sorry, Mum. I'll try to be a better daughter, I really will.'

I'd tried to comfort her, but she'd pulled away from me and stormed upstairs slamming her bedroom door behind her. I had missed Jack so much at that particular time that it physically hurt my heart. This was a time that, if we'd been in Muddleford, I would have run off to our hiding place in the rocks down on the beach. He always knew to find me there and would always wipe away my tears and somehow make me smile. That's why I had loved him so. He had known that Mum was capable of flying into a rage and he made everything feel better. And that's why he would always hold a special place in my heart.

I don't know why those memories had come flooding back that day of all days. Maybe spending time in his company had reminded me that he had been my fixer and my best friend in the whole world. My life-support system. And Mum had taken me away from him.

I hadn't even had time to tell him we were leaving. These days, keeping in touch is so much easier. We could have communicated with each other by text, and never lost touch. It was all so different twenty years ago.

I'd been reading in bed that last night when Mum burst into the room.

'Get up and get dressed, Nell, we're leaving.'

'What? What do you mean leaving?'

'I said get up *now*. Pack your stuff. We're going home.'

'But, Mum, we've only been here a few days

and I'm going out for the day with Jack tomorrow.'

'Not any more you're not, lady. Now do as you are told. Come on.'

There was no reasoning with Mum when she was in one of these moods. She grabbed my wrist and practically dragged me from the bed.

'Mum you're hurting me.'

'Well get a move on then. *Now!*'

'I need to go and tell Jack that we're leaving.'

'You are not going anywhere. You're packing and we're leaving right now. Move it.'

Aunty Lil stood in the doorway to my room. 'Don't leave like this. Let's talk in the morning. We can deal with this. Please, Maria. You're not being fair to Nell.' Her voice wobbled.

'I'm her mother, Lilian. It's about time you realised that Nell is my daughter not yours.'

A loud gasp escaped from Aunty Lil's lips and she clutched her hand to her chest.

'We're leaving, Lilian. And we won't be back *ever*. We're done here. We don't need you in our lives. You've hurt me more than you'll ever know. Come on, Nell. Move it.'

I was as confused as hell, looking from one to the other for answers I wasn't getting. I knew that Mum was in one of her rages and, when she was in them, there was no point in arguing. I stumbled around the room, throwing stuff into my case, not knowing what had gone on between Mum and Aunty Lil. I was so upset that it appeared that my summer holiday had come to an abrupt end. Jack and I had had so many plans. I'd only been here a week and the rest of the school holidays were ahead of us.

Aunty Lil had moved down to the kitchen, and I tried to go in there to talk to her before we left, but Mum wouldn't let me go near her. Not even to say goodbye. I was so torn between these two extremely important women in my life, both of who I had huge love for, and both so influential in their own way.

As Mum's car screeched off the drive, I raised my hand to wave to Aunty Lil. She pressed her hand to the glass, and her forlorn face was forever etched in my mind. That was the last time I saw her.

RELIVING THESE MEMORIES had totally wiped me out. So many feelings that I'd buried deep inside me had risen to the surface. They still hurt as much as they had back then; Mum's drinking, and how she'd said she'd stop after Dad had left us, but that she did it again even when we were trying to make a new life on our own. At the time it had felt as if I wasn't enough for her and that she drank because our life wasn't good enough, that she didn't feel I was worth fighting for and wouldn't stop her drinking. It wasn't until much later that I realised she'd had an illness and as much as she'd tried to stop, and had perhaps wanted to stop, some times more than others, she just couldn't and she'd needed much more help than a sixteen-year-old girl could give her. All I could do was try to make sure she got up for work every morning, was showered, had clean and ironed clothes to wear, and that we had food on the table each night. It wasn't until I met Shivani, that she helped me realise it wasn't my job to do that. That I had been a child, and looking after Mum was too much of a responsibility for me.

Once I went to college, I tried my hardest to keep up with my work as well as keeping on top of everything at home too. I knew of a girl at school who had been taken away from her parents by social services, who had said they weren't capable of looking after her. I wasn't going to let that happen to me and Mum and there was only one of us who was capable of those life skills. Mum needed me to make things right so that she could get through each day.

I wiped a tear from my cheek as these memories churned around inside my head and my grief once again felt unbearable.

I couldn't be bothered to make anything for tea, so after I fed Norman, I curled up on the sofa and mindlessly flicked between TV programmes. Again, I couldn't settle on anything so I grabbed my latest read and disappeared between the pages. Reading had always been one of my escapes from what had been going on in my life. Dorset had been my other.

Aunty Lil had been my safety net. If only she were still here, I could have talked to her. Asked her what happened that night that Mum refused to ever talk about. I should have made more of an effort to keep in touch. Instead of just trying to keep Mum and I afloat and with a roof over our heads. I should have reached out to Aunty Lil. Asked her for her help. Now with both Mum and Aunty Lil gone, I'd never get to the bottom of it all.

Norman, who had taken to sleeping on Aunty Lil's chair, crept over and perched himself at the edge of the sofa. I smiled at him. I felt like we were making progress. He was getting used to me and I was enjoying having some company. This was a huge house to be alone in and having him to chat to made it much more comforting. Him making this small step to be closer to me, meant the world.

'Baby steps, Norman. Baby steps.'

I leaned over to his end of the sofa and stroked his head, looking deep into his gorgeous big brown eyes. Perhaps baby steps were all we were both capable of right now.

Chapter Seventeen

THE RATTLE OF the letterbox and the thud of the local paper landing on the doormat startled me as I was walked through the hallway. I was still in a bit of a sleep daze and hadn't woken up fully. I was sleeping like a log here. A big comfy bed, mixed with sea air and long walks on the beach seemed to be doing me the world of good and within minutes each night I was out for the count.

Flicking on the coffee machine was my new favourite start to the day. I always made sure I got it all ready before I went to bed, so that the aroma of freshly brewed coffee wafted through the whole of the downstairs as one of the first smells of the day. I loved the fact that coffee was ready within seconds, and I could just keep refilling my cup without having to go through the rigmarole of boiling the kettle all the time.

I picked up the paper and went through it page by page, reading every single article. This was as good a place as any to look at what was going on locally and also what sort of work was available should I decide to stay for a short time, or even permanently. I knew, thanks to Aunty Lil, that I didn't need to worry about money for a while, but I wasn't sure whether the life of a lady of leisure would suit me. I thought it might be nice at first but after a few days, I reckoned I'd be bored stiff. I was only thirty-four and I'd never not had a job since I left college. I could hardly retire. People would think I was a right lazy cow! Maybe part-time was an option. Then I could enjoy the local area and take Norman for lots of lovely long walks without trying to cram them in around a full day of work, which would probably feel like more of a chore. The more I thought about that, the more I liked the idea. Then I could spend time at the beach hut too. Even take up running, which was something I'd wanted to do for a while but didn't seem to have the time or the energy, or both, for.

I stood and stretched. The view from the lounge window was so stunning, I'd moved the furniture around slightly – moving Aunty Lil's chair to the other side of the window and another armchair in the best spot to admire the view. The sea had always soothed me when I was a child and it still did. It was simply captivating to gaze at and

I'm sure I'd already lost so much time doing so since I'd been here.

But sitting and staring at the sea, wasn't helping to find me a job.

'Come on Nellie. Crack on.' I needed to give myself a kick up the backside.

Returning to the paper, I smiled as I skimmed the local interest stories, particularly those that were charity- or animal-related. I didn't pay much attention to the local paper at home. Most weeks it came straight through the front door and back out in the wheelie bin because I never seemed to find the time to read it, although I now perhaps thought I didn't *make* the time. We can all say we don't have time, but we *can* make the time to do the things that we really want to do. It never ceased to amaze me when people would say they didn't have time to do things they really wanted to, but would religiously sit down to watch endless hours of TV each day. Perhaps that was their relaxation but you can't have it all ways. You have to change something, if you want something to change.

It seemed there was quite a local community here, with stories about fun days and school projects. I noticed an ad for the dog socialising event that Jack had mentioned and ripped it out, placing it on the windowsill. It *was* something I'd like to go to. Meet some new people. Maybe make some new friends. It would be good for me and Norman.

Glancing across at Norman, I wondered what he was thinking. He still seemed to mope around a lot. He must have missed Aunty Lil. I hoped that he'd be happy with me. If we did move back up to the Midlands I would definitely have to find some nice places to walk him; he was used to walking on a lovely sandy beach. There was Cannock Chase Forest, which I'd been to a few times in the past, and where I knew a lot of people took their dogs and it's always looked really lovely. It was definitely something for the 'going home' side of the list.

A huge advertisement for the local regatta which was happening in a few weeks jumped out of the centre pages. Oh how I had loved that event as a child. Aunty Lil used to take us every summer and it was such fun. I remembered a local, all-male brass band, dressed in smart white trousers, with starched white shirts, red-and-white stripy blazers and straw hats, always played music from the bandstand in the middle of the park. The park was full of fairground stalls of all sorts, games to play, trampolines to bounce on. Food stalls galore lined the streets too. My favourite was always the van that sold hot sugary doughnuts. Divine. As we got older, Jack and I were allowed to wander around on our own and then meet Aunty Lil later where we would sit on picnic blankets and enjoy the extravagant firework display, which was always such an amazing end to the day.

That was definitely something I'd love to relive. I took my diary from my handbag and scribbled in the date of the event. It would be great to do that with Jack for old time's sake, I thought, but I assumed he would be going with Natalia. Anyway, it was about time I started to make new memories. I had to stop living in the past if I was going to make it work out here, even if it was only short term, so perhaps I would be brave and go alone. Or Norman could be my date for the night instead.

I wondered what was happening at home. I didn't have that many friends, mainly the people I worked with. Shivani was my bestie and had been for the last eighteen years after we'd met at college. I took business studies and she was taking hairdressing and beauty. I first saw her on one of the first few days after I'd got my lunch and was wondering where to sit. Everyone seemed to be in groups and I was so self-conscious, not knowing a soul and with my confidence and self-esteem still taking a knocking from the bullying in high school.

I glanced over and thought how gorgeous her jet-black, lustrous hair was. Poker straight and glossier than I'd ever seen. It was a total contrast to my fine, mousy-brown lifeless mop which had no shape at all and never shone. It made me so envious.

There was one empty table, and the table that this girl was sat at. I could sit on the empty table alone or I could make an effort to get to know new people, so I took a deep breath and wandered over to hers.

'Err... Excuse me. Do you mind if I sit here?' I almost whispered.

As she looked up, I saw that her eyes were red and she'd been crying.

'Oh gosh, I'm sorry. Are you OK?'

'Please sit, but only if you are not going to poke fun at me. I've just about had enough of everyone today.'

I noticed that she had the most beautiful voice that changed tone with every word, almost sing-songy.

'I really won't. I'm Nell by the way.' I reached across and held out my hand to shake hers.

She smiled. She had the most beautiful huge dark-brown eyes and lustrous long lashes to die for.

'Thank you! I'm Shivani. Do you mind me asking, why you wanted to sit by me?'

'Oh I'm so sorry. Am I interrupting you and all your invisible friends having a great time?' I asked defensively.

'Ha! Hardly. I'm the girl with the dark-coloured skin who no-one wants to sit with.'

'Oh you have darker skin? I hadn't noticed.'

I smiled and the corners of her mouth twitched and those stunning eyes started to sparkle.

Shivani told me she was on a hairdressing and beauty course but all the other girls in the course were white and seemed to treat her differently. They'd all paired up quickly, seemingly not wanting to partner her, and she'd been left the last one standing and had to work with the tutor, which they'd all sniggered at.

I smiled.

'Don't laugh at me.' She raised her voice.

'Oh I'm not laughing, I promise. I was smiling at your voice, it's so colourful and interesting. I love it. I'm really not laughing. Trust me, I know what it's like to be treated differently. I spent the last few weeks at high school being bullied and I wouldn't do that to another soul. I'd have been the first one to pair up with you.'

'Really? You don't mind what colour my skin is?'

'Couldn't care less. Tell those spiteful girls that if they're nasty to you, they'll have us both to deal with. Bitches! But what you can do, is tell me how I can get my hair to look as lush as yours. If you need someone to practice your hairdressing and beauty on, then... tadah!' I stretched out my arms. 'I'm your girl.'

We chatted easily over lunch and discovered that we would be taking the same bus home so went our separate ways to classes and arranged to meet up at the end of the day to travel home together. Shivani seemed to hold her head a little higher as she headed off to her first class of the afternoon and I felt a little lighter in the hope that I might just have made the first proper friend I'd made in years.

Who would have guessed eighteen years ago that we'd end up working for the same company and being with each other nearly every day. She'd been such a good friend to me over the years. We'd gone through so much together. She and her wonderful family had helped me through some of my darkest moments, when Mum had become worse and worse and when I could do no more to help and her drinking finally became the thing that took her away from me.

Mrs Sharma, who was not only an incredible

cook, but also a feeder, constantly sent Shivani round to my house with cartons of food because she wanted to make sure my freezer was stocked full and that I wouldn't go hungry. One of the other things she was amazing at was hugs. The sort of hugs where someone really takes you in their arms and holds you like they just want to make everything better. Those type of hugs that warm your heart were not things I'd had from my own mum for a very long time. The Sharmas were a huge part of my life and my past, I knew that if I did move here permanently that I would miss them dearly.

A tear trickled down my cheek, as their absence made my heart hurt right then. I popped Shivani a short message to see if she was around later for a chat. I hoped that I could persuade her to come and see me really soon to help me make some really life-changing decisions. I hadn't made a decision without going over and over it with her for many years. I needed her help. Maybe she could come down for the regatta weekend. That would definitely make it fun. The thought bucked me up a little. Yes, I would definitely suggest that when we caught up.

Chapter Eighteen

THE THING ABOUT not having a job to get up for every day, and nothing really to do is that you lose any sort of structure in your life. All I'd done that day so far was drink coffee and read the paper. And I had no other plans. It felt weird. The having no plans. I really didn't know what to do with myself. Both short- and long-term. The only thing in my diary that week was to go to the funeral directors the next day with Dom. He'd been very kind and had text me every day to make sure I was OK. He'd obviously made a promise to Aunty Lil to keep an eye on me, but he really did seem very thoughtful.

'Come on, Norm, shall we go for a walk?'

Norman's ears perked up and as he looked at me, he tilted his head, first one way, then the other. He was such a cutie and always made me smile. I grabbed his lead from the hall table, clipped it to his collar, then picked up the ball flinger I'd found in the cupboard under the stairs the day before. He ran to the front door and danced on all fours in anticipation.

We crossed the road to the beach, which was practically deserted. Once on the sand, I felt nervous about letting him off the lead on my own. When Jack was with me, I felt he was the one who knew Norman better and what the dog was capable of. I supposed a practically empty beach was as good a place as any for me to try things on my own. I just had to be brave and have confidence in myself and Norman. We had to learn to trust each other.

Taking Jack's advice, I had brought the small tin of dog treats I'd been using at home to reward Norman. I'd shake it when Norman was in the garden and I wanted him to come in, so he knew the noise well. This was our moment!

'Come on, Norman. We've got this!' I let him off the lead and held my breath. My heart was pounding.

The minute he was let loose, he scampered off down to the sea and dipped his toes in the water. I shook the tin and he turned and looked at me, and then back at the sea. I shook it again and called his name in the way Jack had told me to. He'd said if you shout, angrily or panicking, the dog will know they're in trouble and it could be a problem getting them back, so I shouted it in my jolliest tone. I felt like a complete tit, to be honest, however, he came immediately back and sat at my feet.

'Oh, Norman, you are such a good boy.' I crouched down to his level. Jack had taught me to do this so that I wasn't not talking down to him. 'Good boy!' I said it in a over-enthusiastic and happy voice. Jack said it made dogs know they had pleased you and that most dogs just wanted to please their owner.

He'd also said that Norman was quite ball obsessed and should come back when I threw a ball. I got Norman to stay by my side while I flung the ball across the beach. He ran after it excitedly and brought it straight back to me. We went through the whole process of me praising him again and he seemed to be really enjoying himself. We repeated this process what felt like a million times, but watching him be so happy warmed my heart. The poor little thing had been through a lot lately. He'd seen Aunty Lil die in front of him, had been taken to stay next door while they waited for me to come down, then been thrown into the same house he'd lived in, but with a new person. Every night he slept outside of Aunty Lil's bedroom door, which I'd kept shut. The poor little mite mustn't know what was going on. I wondered what was going on in his head and whether he realised she was never coming back.

'Come on, mate. Let's go and get a drink. I think we deserve one.'

We headed up to the café and took one of the seats outside. It felt good to feel the warm sun on my face. When the waitress came over to take my order, my tummy rumbled loudly and we both laughed. Looking at my watch and realising it was already 11.30 and I'd not had any breakfast, I ordered a toasted teacake to go with my latte. There were a few people dotted around at various tables but it was reasonably quiet. Norman leaned up against my leg under the table. Another step. This was the closest he'd physically been to me. Progress again. I smiled down at him and tickled behind his ears and he looked up at me and I was sure he grinned. My heart felt full, which was different to how it had felt for a long time.

Back at home after filling my face, I decided to pick up my pen and pad and walk round the house to make some – objective! – notes about each room and what I'd do if I stayed or what would have to be got rid of if I sold the house. There were so many rooms in the house that I'd only poked my head around the door of since I'd arrived. And I did like a list. I think because it let me procrastinate about the actual thing I should have been doing, by making a list about it. It kind of gave me permission to procrastinate.

I decided to tackle the library first. It was the room I used to spend most of my time in when I was younger. Norman pottered in behind me and curled up into a ball on the bed settee. I brushed my fingers against the dusty spines of all the classic novels lined up on the shelves. Dickens, Emily Bronte, Jane Austin, Charlotte Bronte and CS Lewis were the names that I recognised the most. And so many volumes of the Encyclopaedia Britannica too. I remembered doing my school-holiday projects in this room with all the encyclopaedias spread on the floor around me. They all looked so beautifully at home in this glorious room of dark wooden shelves and flock wallpaper.

A dark wooden desk sat in the middle of the room and I sat down in the old-fashioned leather chair. The desk overlooked the front garden and I wasn't entirely sure if this was a desk you were meant to write at, or just admire the view. Beyond the beautiful plants there was the turquoise sea which was shimmering under the sun. Perhaps it was a view that should inspire you to write. I swore I could still sit in the library for hours and hours. It had felt like such a grown-up room when

I was younger, so warm and inviting, at a time when I was between being a girl and growing into my body and the emotions that went into maturing into a young woman. The winged back leather armchair and footstool that I always used to curl up in next to the window now sat in the corner under a reading light and a mohair throw was arranged neatly over the back of the chair. Looking around, I breathed it all in. I still adored it and there was not one thing I would change in this room!

I was off to a good start. I flung open the window to air the room and sprayed some air freshener around to get rid of the fusty smell of the books.

'Come on, Norm. Let's go.'

Instead of closing the door when I left, I propped it open with a doorstop. This was not a room to be hidden away.

I decided that the next room to tackle was going to be Aunty Lil's room. This was going to be the hardest emotionally. Norman trotted in behind me and jumped up onto the bed snuggling into the pillows. Bless him. I knew that Aunty Lil's cleaner had been in the day after Lil had passed away. The cleaner had changed the bedclothes and dusted and vacuumed the whole house, but I'm sure the bed still smelled of Lil. The room certainly did. I breathed in and hoped that I would never forget that smell.

Opening the wardrobe, I started to look through her clothes. When I was younger I'd thought Aunty Lil was a bit like the queen as she always very well put together, modern for her age – matching twinsets and skirts at times, very rarely seen in a pair of trousers but normally in lovely dresses that used to swish this way and that. I'd always dreamt that when I grew up I wanted to be stylish just like Aunty Lil. It used to annoy Mum when I said that, but Mum was far from stylish.

Aunty Lil once said that style was a feeling rather than a look and that your clothes should make you feel happy. I was glad that memory came back to me then. It was something I had forgotten over the years, dressing for myself rather than the occasion. From now on I would only wear clothes that made me feel happy.

My aunt always spent a lot of money on clothes and would only buy from the best local dressmakers. She'd loved treating me to new clothes too; she'd known how much Mum had struggled for money. I suddenly remembered an argument that she and Mum had, when Mum had told her to stop dressing me up like a doll and had pointed out that I was not her daughter. Now I knew that she had lost her own daughter, it all made a lot more sense. I wished that they hadn't kept it from me at the time.

There was a little part of me that hoped I'd find something that might tell me why my mother and aunt had argued. Why our lives had had to change so much. Maybe I'd find a box of letters, or a diary even. Something that would explain. There was nothing obvious though, no hidden boxes on top of, or at the back of the drawers or wardrobes. Maybe Dom might know something, I thought. Perhaps I could ask him the next time I saw him.

Aunt Lil had some beautiful dresses and there were some in this wardrobe that would be classed as proper vintage. I took out a gorgeous green-and-blue mottled taffeta dress with a full skirt and a fitted bodice and held it up against me. I reckoned it was around my size and on a whim decided to try it on. I smoothed it over my hips and fluffed out the skirt. It felt amazing and fitted perfectly. It was a dress that deserved to be danced in along with a dance partner who would look deep into his partner's eyes as he twirled them around.

I floated down the stairs and flicked on the radio on the hall table. I twiddled with the knobs until I tuned into 'Moon River' by Andy Williams. Ah, this was one of Aunty Lil's favourite songs, how perfect, as if it was sent from heaven above. The vocals were warm and dreamy and I sashayed around the hall with my eyes closed, twirling and twirling and singing along.

As I sang the final words, I realised it wasn't just my voice singing along, but another deeper voice that certainly didn't belong to Andy Williams. I slowly opened one eye and groaned as I opened the other. Leaning against the kitchen door frame was Jack, who was grinning at me from ear to ear. I couldn't help but smile back at him even though I was mortified that he'd seen me like this.

'Back door was open. Sorry to disturb you. I heard the music and did shout your name, but you obviously couldn't hear me, so I took the liberty of coming through. Hope that's OK. I was just home for lunch and wondered how you were today and whether you'd consider coming along to the socialising class tonight. It starts at 7 p.m. at the vet's. I could swing by and pick you and young Norman here up about quarter to. What do you think? Unless you are staying in with your imaginary dance partner that is.' He winked.

My face flushed. 'I'd love to. Give me a minute and I'll just go and get changed and we can sort everything out. Help yourself to a coffee.'

'OK cool. Oh and by the way, Nellie-bum.'

'Yes?'

He strode over to me and lifted his hand to my face, tenderly tucking a stray strand of hair behind my ear. He was so close that I could feel his warm breath on my face. I looked up into his beautiful eyes. He was gorgeous. My Jack. I felt a rush of emotion, which almost completely overwhelmed me. Would I ever think of him as anything but mine?

'You look absolutely stunning in that dress. I have to confess I watched you for a minute or two. You were mesmerising. I couldn't take my eyes off you.'

His eyes slid down to my lips and then back to my eyes. I bit my lip and gasped as I knew in that moment he was about to kiss me. And right then, I wanted him to so much. He leaned closer and his lips were mere millimetres from mine. He took my face gently in his hands. I closed my eyes.

Then an image of Natalia flashed into my mind, and stopped me in my tracks, and I took a swift step back.

My face turned puce and I rubbed the back of my neck as I muttered 'thank you' and ran upstairs as quickly as I could. I slammed the bedroom door behind me and stood against it breathing heavily and fanning myself with my hands. I didn't know how to act when he said those things to me and looked at me in that way. I'd dreamt of hearing them all those years ago.

But I didn't know if he was teasing me and playfully flirting or whether he really liked me – even though he hadn't known the real me for the last twenty years. I wasn't sure whether my thirty-four-year-old self was handling this any better than my fourteen-year-old-self handled things all those years ago.

I was going to have to tackle this situation somehow. I knew that if he carried on behaving in this way, I couldn't be responsible for my actions.

Chapter Nineteen

WHEN I CAME down after getting changed Jack had gone and there was a hastily scribbled note on the hall table saying: 'SOZ. HAD TO GO. PICK YOU UP AT 6.45.'

At least I didn't have to worry immediately about how to handle things between us. I looked at my watch. It was 1.30. I would fill another few hours going through Aunty Lil's wardrobe. There was nothing else I needed to be doing and it would help to keep my mind off how Jack had made me feel.

The afternoon flew by and I had a wonderful time sorting her clothes out into piles. There were some glorious garments that I really wanted to keep for myself, but also many that were the wrong size for me. I'd have to find somewhere to take them, I thought.

A memory popped into my mind of Aunty Lil taking us to local jumble sales. Mum would always turn up her nose at the thought, but Aunty Lil's jumble sales were not normal. They were much more upper class with lots of rich older women selling clothes that most of the time still had labels attached. Perhaps I'd ask around and see whether they still happened. I could pop round to Val's. Jack would be at work so at least I wouldn't have to worry about bumping into him and I'm sure his mum wouldn't mind me asking her.

When I popped over and tapped on the open back door, Val covered up whatever she'd been doing with a tea towel.

'Are you icing cakes?'

'Oh yes, you caught me! I was going to ice them and bring some round to you later. They're not the best though so I didn't want anyone to see them.'

I couldn't believe they weren't anything but perfect. Val was an amazing baker!

I'd spent a lovely hour with Val over a pot of tea. We'd chatted about how Aunty Lil had been over the last few years and she'd been really kind when I got a little upset at the fact that I'd not seen her for so long and then lost my chance.

'Sweetheart, everything happens for a reason. We don't always know what that reason is. We were all surprised and incredibly sad when your mum took you both off in the middle of the night,

Jack especially, but we all also knew that your mum was tackling her own demons at the time and was doing her best. That's all you can ask from someone. You were just a child and had to go along with your mum's decision.

'I suppose what we didn't know then was that all ties would be cut. You can't change the past, my darling, but you can look forward and enjoy the future.' She reached out and took my hand in hers. 'All I'll say is don't spoil the future by worrying about how you could have done things differently in the past. You have the chance at a new life here in a place you have always loved and if you'd like to try to live that life, we're all here to help you. You know that Jack adores you and would do anything for you.'

I smiled at her through my tears.

'And if you decide that you want to go back to the Midlands, then that's fine too. Or you could flit between the two. Whatever happens, we are together once more. It's wonderful to have you back in our lives and we're here for you.'

I came back from Val's with a full heart, less guilt and a list of places to ask about donating or selling Aunty Lil's clothes. There was a swishing shop back home that I could always go to if I couldn't find anywhere else in this neck of the woods. A friend of mine had introduced me to 'Rita's Rags to Riches' a couple of years ago. It was a fabulous find. You took your clothes along and swapped them for others and if you wanted anything additional you just paid Rita a nominal fee. Word had spread and people came from miles away and loved it so much that they, in turn, recommended it to others.

An idea started to form in my head. I wondered whether I could set up a local swishing event with some of Aunty Lil's clothes. It wouldn't be treading on Rita's toes, because she was so far away, and I was sure if I popped in to see her, she'd give me some tips too. She was a lovely lady. I could check out some local venues and see if there might be any interest. It would give me something to talk about at the dog event that night – putting the feelers out.

I wondered if something like this might even be of interest to Natalia. While I was pretty sure she'd never dream of buying second-hand clothes, her being so glamorous could make her a great help and maybe she'd have some friends she could invite along. I made a mental note to ask Jack for her contact details. Maybe it would bring us closer together. When we got to know each other better perhaps we could even be friends. I just had to get over my little crush on her fiancé, which seemed to have resurrected itself after twenty years. Just a minor point.

Jack knocked on the back door at dead on 6.45. I couldn't quite meet his eye as we walked out to his pickup truck. He lifted Norman up onto the back seat and I could probably have done with a bunk-up myself as my performance of getting into the vehicle wasn't my most elegant moment.

The vet's practice was less than a ten-minute drive away. We pulled through the gates and down a long driveway, into an impressive stable yard, and parked outside the building at the far side of the complex. Jack jumped out of the truck and came round to open my door. Static electricity made us both jump back, before he gave me a hand down, grinning at me. I couldn't help but grin back. As I turned round to head inside I saw Natalia glaring at me out of a window. She came out and greeted Jack with a kiss on his cheek, leaving a lipstick imprint which I'm sure was intended. When I asked her if I could have a word with her later, because I was after her help, she actually preened and I wondered if maybe she was one of those people who need to feel needed and that this was my 'in' with her. I considered that at some point, too, I might have to tell her that she had nothing to worry about with Jack and that he was just being nice to me for old time's sake. Maybe then we'd start to bond.

The people attending the socialising night were of all ages and there was a multitude of dog sizes and varieties from Chihuahuas to Poodles, Cockapoos, Labradors, Rottweilers and some very bouncy Spaniels. We all sat in a circle in the large function room at the back of the surgery. It was a great space and it did make me wonder whether it might be a good place to hold my event. My mind was working overtime as I wondered whether I could book the room for a small fee and maybe also market it to the vet's clientele. I'd have a chat with Jack about it on the way home.

Jack hadn't mentioned that it was him who took the class. We discussed the legalities and good practices of having a dog, and he went through doggy first aid and some basic training methods. He got the dogs and owners in a circle together in the middle of the room and made us keep walking past each other. This would help the dogs socialise.

The hour passed really quickly and when everyone had left Jack asked me if I minded hanging around while he grabbed some stuff from the office. Natalia popped her head around the door and noticed I was in the room alone and came and sat beside me.

She smiled, but it didn't reach her eyes.

'Can we do lunch, Nellie?'

I cringed. I wished she wouldn't call me that. That was for people who knew me really well.

'Are you free tomorrow? You said you needed my help and there're some things that I think you and I need to talk about too, don't you?'

My face flushed again. I explained that Dom was coming tomorrow to sort out the final funeral arrangements so we planned for the next day instead. She nodded towards the door as Jack strode across to join us and told Natalia that he'd see her the next day. She asked me to leave them alone for a moment, Jack huffed and threw his keys at me, and Norman and I went to wait in the car. At least it didn't matter how ungainly I mounted the vehicle this time.

Two minutes later, Jack flung open his car door and jumped in.

I told him I was having lunch with Natalia the day after next and he grimaced and told me to take everything she said with a pinch of salt. He was very quiet on the journey home and even though I tried hard to keep the conversation going, it felt very one way. It was very different to the way he'd been over the last few days. I hoped I hadn't done something to upset him. Whenever Callum behaved like that, it was always something I'd done. Or so he'd said. Most of the time I'd walked around on eggshells trying to make sure he was happy. Though it hadn't really occurred to me until then in the car.

Gazing out the window, the more I thought about mine and Callum's relationship, the more I wondered whether it had actually been very healthy. He'd seemed to not even like me that much most of the time; picking at me constantly about the things I did and the things I said. Why we were even getting married? I supposed when you were in the middle of a relationship, you didn't notice the things that you noticed after-wards. You thought that because you were in a relationship with someone, that the way they behaved was OK and you just accepted it. Some-one constantly picking away at you knocks your confidence and your self-esteem. But when it's someone who is meant to love you doing it, and it's gradual, you don't seem to notice for some reason. I hadn't realised until I'd taken a step back from it all how Callum's behaviour had made me feel at the time.

I thought of Aunty Lil and wondered whether she'd have accepted that type of behaviour, and I knew the answer straightaway.

Jack walked Norman and I to the gate. He was still really quiet although he did give me a peck on the cheek. Perhaps this 'thing' I had for him would disappear quickly if we carried on this way. Perhaps it was actually safer for him to behave this way for both of our sakes. That way he could get on with his life with Natalia and I could make some decisions about my future too.

Chapter Twenty

THE FUNERAL DIRECTOR introduced himself as William as he shook my hand. He was a small man, with kind eyes, and he immediately put me at ease, talking about Aunty Lil with much respect and as if he knew her well.

Dom had been in to see him beforehand and had organised most of the things that Aunty Lil had left instructions about. She'd been quite specific, which had taken a lot of the pressure off me. She'd already chosen her casket, some music and where she wanted her get-together (she didn't want to call it a wake) to be, and Dom had very kindly already made the provisional arrangements. The funeral was confirmed for the following Monday at 11 a.m. All that was really left to do was to drop in any clothes that I wanted her to wear, unless I wanted her in one of the gowns that they could provide, along with anything else I wanted to include in the coffin. I had no clue what that might be, if anything, but promised to give it some thought and to return on Friday with some clothing. I didn't want her in a gown. I thought she should wear something very special.

William had asked me whether I wanted to see Aunty Lil, but I couldn't bring myself to. Memories flooded back to when I'd had to organise Mum's funeral. I'd insisted on seeing her and had regretted it ever since. She hadn't looked like my mum. She'd looked dead, which obviously I knew she would, but she looked like a doll version of my mum in the sort of gown-cum-nightie that she wouldn't have wanted to have been seen dead in. Literally.

The funeral itself had been a quiet affair and Shivani and her family were there holding my hand through the whole process. At just seventeen years old, it was the worst thing I'd ever had to do. Drink had stolen my mother from me. She was way too young to die and I was way too young to have been left alone. I spent a long time being angry with her and it tore me up inside.

I'd found a letter with my father's phone number in it, which she'd clearly hidden from me, and I'd plucked up the courage to ring him. He'd told me in no uncertain terms that he wasn't prepared to come to the funeral and asked me not to contact him or his family ever again. He'd said he had a new family and he didn't want them upset by his past catching up with him. I was totally and utterly devasted. He couldn't even be there for me. His own flesh and blood. I'd vowed then that I would never have anything to do with him again.

It wasn't until I went to counselling, which Shivani's wonderful mum insisted that I went to, that I started to make some sense of it all and began to forgive my mother and to see the demon drink as an illness she had no control over.

I shook my head now to try to shake away the memories because I still, all these years on, found them hard to deal with.

DOM'S JAGUAR GLIDED to a stop outside a pub that was only a short drive from the village. The freshly painted name sign was swinging in the breeze. It had been called The Fisherman's Haunt and we'd gone there for lunches years ago, but now it was called the Cock Inn. I knew it was childish of me, but I couldn't help but smile at the name. I'm sure Aunty Lil had chosen it on purpose for her 'get-together'. It was typical of her sense of humour. Being there brought back lots of happy memories but at the same time it seemed sad to be holding her get-together there.

Mary and Bill Potter, the landlady and her husband, were such a lovely couple and were so kind to us when we made all the final arrangements that I knew it was all going to be OK and bearable. It just seemed odd that I'd be going to her funeral and wouldn't know that many people there. She'd had a whole life without me over these last two decades, that I knew nothing of, although I was looking forward to learning all about it.

Lunch itself was really lovely. Dom was so easy to chat with, such good company. Not the stuffy, uptight person I thought he was when we'd first spoken. He talked about his friendship with Jack, that they'd been at university together and how wonderfully accepting and supportive he had been when Dom had announced his sexuality. Hearing more about Jack from someone else who knew him was wonderful.

'And do you like Natalia?' I asked casually. 'She seems nice.'

'All I'll say is that Natalia is not always as she seems. I won't speak ill of the girl, and I'm not one to gossip, but just be wary, Nell, that's all I'll say.'

I found Dom's advice very interesting. But I didn't want to ask any more at that point, and reminded myself that Jack's choice of partner was up to him.

I mentioned the swishing idea to Dom. I thought he'd be a sensible person to talk business with and he said that he thought it was a cracking idea and that Aunty Lil would have been absolutely delighted with my decision. When I talked about a venue, he said that he was sure the right place would come to me when I was looking around and that he trusted me to make a great choice.

When he dropped me back at the house I realised I'd forgotten to ask him if he knew anything about the falling out between Mum and Aunty Lil. I went back up to Aunty Lil's room, annoyed with myself for not remembering, and worked through more of her stuff. There were two other wardrobes in the other bedrooms too, stuffed full of clothes. It was such a delight to go through them all, imagining where she might have gone in them, and what she might have done. There were loads of pretty dresses that I couldn't wait to try on and still another growing pile of items that I either knew wouldn't suit me, or wouldn't fit me. I picked up a green-and-orange taffeta party dress and held it against my body. The bodice would be a snug fit but the overskirt and net underskirt would make it look absolutely stunning. I swung from side to side and imagined Aunty Lil being whirled around by a handsome partner as she danced under the moonlight. Old-fashioned dancing was so romantic. Maybe he would have dipped her backwards and leaned in for a kiss.

Yapping brought me back to the present.

'Oh Norman, what's up?'

He circled around himself, which was normally a sign that he wanted to go out. I looked at my watch and couldn't believe it was nearly 8 p.m. I'd been upstairs for hours. I laid the dress back on the spare bed and he trotted alongside me across the landing before running full pelt down the stairs and wagging his tail against the floor tiles. I ruffled his head as I got close and he nuzzled into my hand. We were definitely becoming friends and I surprised myself by how much I enjoyed his company. Who needed a man in their life? Perhaps Norman *was* all I really needed.

We'd been for another walk along the beach first thing that morning and that time I hadn't been so anxious about letting him off the lead, and he'd been golden and came back to make sure I was still there too every so often. He really was a pleasure to look after. There was a woodland area at the bottom of Larkspur Lane, but we hadn't ventured that way yet, favouring the beach every time. Maybe when I got used to being by the sea, we'd explore other walks too. We'd walked back through the village for a change. It was only small, but there were two pretty rows of shops with brightly-coloured bunting which draped from one side of the street to the other. The shops that I noticed the most were those which were quite practical – a trendy-looking hairdresser, a bakery which had the most delicious-looking cakes and pastries in their bay window, a butcher, an off-licence and a couple of others that I couldn't quite see what they were. As we walked past the final shop in the left-hand row, an attractive blonde lady came out wearing a tabard and Norman pulled on the lead to get to her, eagerly wagging his tail.

'Hello, dear, you must be Nell. And as you can see, I already know Norman. I'm Pamela.'

I gave a little wave and looked up at the sign above to see what type of shop it was. Pamela's Pet Shop and Pampered Pooches. No wonder they knew Norman.

'I was so sorry to hear about Lilian, my dear. Such a loss to the local community, she was such a wonderful soul. Always had time for everyone. A real gem. She'll be sadly missed.' She felt around in her tabard pockets and asked if it was OK to give Norman a treat.

'Thank you, and of course.'

'But we're all delighted that you've come down to spend some time here. Do you know whether you'll stay or not?'

Crikey. Talk about getting straight to the point.

'I'm not going anywhere in the immediate future but obviously there's lots to think about.'

'Well, we'll be seeing you on Monday at the funeral, my dear. It's going to be a sad day but a good one too. You'll get to meet lots of Lilian's friends and hopefully learn more about her through them. It really has been lovely to meet you. Lilian loved you dearly and talked about you often.' Pamela reached across and squeezed my hand.

Her words had surprised me. I'd thought that Aunty Lil might not have mentioned us to her friends, but I suppose they might have been around to pick up the pieces after we'd left that night.

I'd asked Pamela for a business card. She'd told she usually groomed Norman every couple of months, and that she could keep delivering his pet food too. It made sense to me not to change anything. She'd seemed lovely. And perhaps she'd be able to give me some tips about how to look after Norman.

I'd never have chosen to have a dog, but there were worse things than having one thrust on you at very short notice. I had wondered at first if I'd be lonely in Aunty Lil's big old house on my own, but I found having Norman around was lovely! He was good company and didn't answer back. The perfect male companion.

Chapter Twenty-One

I SPENT LONGER choosing an outfit to wear for lunch with Natalia than I did choosing my wedding dress – which reminded me that I needed to crack on with the cancellation list for the wedding. Eventually I settled on a pair of fitted black trousers, a white chiffon camisole, a sparkly belt and some silver ballet flats. A black blazer with three-quarter sleeves would look smart but casual. As I looked this way and that in the bedroom mirror, I decided that I looked pretty presentable, even though the outfit didn't particularly bring me joy, but perhaps that was more about where I was going and who with.

As I walked out of Aunty Lil's room, a multi-coloured silk scarf hanging on the back of the door caught my eye. I tied it around my neck in an air-hostess style, and it definitely bought a little brightness to the outfit. I'd seen someone wearing something similar on TV recently, and thought that it looked elegant yet simple.

Slicking on some black mascara, giving my cheeks a little brush over with some bronzer and slathering on a little natural-coloured lip gloss, I reminded myself that I wasn't, and couldn't ever compare or compete with, Natalia. If Jack had chosen her to be his wife, then that was his decision, and I needed to let Natalia know that I would really like to get to know her better and be her friend as well as his, and that I would be happy for them. Yes, I would. Perhaps I needed to work on my convincing face. I just needed to work through the feelings I had for him. They were just childhood emotions that had resurfaced with seeing him again and were playing havoc with my mind. Yes, that's what they were.

Natalia had sent me a text message the day before and had suggested meeting at the café on the quay. She was already there when I arrived. I could spot her fuscia-coloured lipstick from the door. She stood to greet me, kissing me on both cheeks like we were old friends. Her perfume was really overpowering and tickled the back of my throat. She was most pleasant at first, asking how I'd got on with Dom yesterday. Though after I'd ordered chicken, ham and leek pie and chips for lunch, she ordered a Caesar salad which I'm sure she did on purpose to make me feel like a big fat greedy pig.

'If I have a cooked meal now, I won't have to cook later,' I excused myself, knowing full well that I'd probably stuff my face with a Chinese takeaway for tea later. But she didn't need to know that. I did like my food and my size-16 figure reflected that. Natalia's perfect size-10 figure and permanent scowl reflected that she probably needed a good pie for lunch instead of a salad.

'I'm sure you've wondered why I've invited you out to lunch, Nellie.'

God, the way she said my name really grated. I smiled sweetly.

'I thought we should clear the air over the' – she made speech marks in the air – 'Jack situation.'

'The Jack situation?' I questioned. 'I didn't realise there was a situation.' I was starting to feel hot so I loosened the silk scarf around my neck.

'Well, Nellie, the way you keep fawning over him and looking at him with those big puppy-dog eyes of yours really has to stop.' She paused for effect and linked her hands together, resting her head on the bridge she'd made.

I gulped.

'I hate to see any woman making a fool of themselves and that's exactly what you are doing, Nellie. Fluttering your eyelashes at him and giving him those long lingering looks are not going to get you anywhere. Jack has asked me not to say anything to you, but I felt that I must. I know that I can trust you to keep it to yourself. I can, can't I?'

I nodded nervously, looked down and fiddled with my bracelet.

'The truth is, Nellie, he's embarrassed by your behaviour!'

God Natalia, break it to me gently why don't you?

'He feels that he *has* to spend time with you when he really doesn't want to and, quite frankly, he doesn't have the time anyway, what with his very important job and spending time with me too. And of course, there's all the wedding plans we're making. He's going to be a married man very soon. You really shouldn't embarrass him or yourself in this way.'

Heat rose up my body and my face felt like it was on fire. I've never been more mortified in my life. I felt like I was back at school with those girls being spiteful and bitchy towards me. So much so that my defence mechanisms kicked in for a short while and I squared my shoulders and took a deep breath.

'I'm not sure what you think is going on, Natalia, but I can assure you that my intentions towards Jack are purely as a friend and nothing else. We share a history and that's it. I feel nothing else towards him. And certainly nothing that you are implying.' It hurt my heart to say these words but I knew that I had to lie here for self-preservation.

'Well history should stay in the past, Nellie,' said Natalia. 'That's why it's called history. It has no place here. Jack has enough friends in his life and doesn't need any more. He told me that he didn't know how to tell you this without upsetting you, so I've done it for him. That's what life partners do. They look out for each other. Don't you agree?'

For the next however long I had to sit there and be pleasant to her while I tried to eat my lunch. There had been no consideration for my feelings whatsoever. She launched into her wedding plans, even though I knew she knew that Callum and I had recently had to cancel our wedding. Talk about rubbing my nose in it. She told me how she and Jack were planning to get married later that summer, in a big stately home and have the reception in a huge marquee in the grounds. She didn't seem to be able to shut up talking and didn't even notice that I wasn't that interested. I just hoped that I nodded in all the right places.

I was surprised that Val hadn't mentioned anything to me about the wedding. Nor Jack neither. But then she mentioned that one of the reasons no-one knew anything yet was that Jack wanted to make a huge announcement at the regatta this year about their engagement and wedding plans to surprise everyone, including his parents, and he wanted to keep it a secret until then. She made me promise to not even tell Jack that I knew anything because he'd made her agree to not telling a soul and he'd be annoyed with her if he knew that she'd shared it with anyone, and especially me of all people. Charming.

This was one of the worst experiences of my life. It made the thought of cancelling the rest of my own wedding plans an absolute walk in the park. I decided that when I got home I would get through as many of those little jobs I'd been putting off for as long as I could.

Natalia pushed her food around her plate rather than ate anything. I wasn't sure whether she was just doing it to try to make me look bad, or whether it was her normal eating habit. Pushing my plate to one side, desperate to get away from this awful situation, I made my excuses. As I stood to leave, she held her arms out to me and leaned in for a hug. I didn't get a choice of whether I wanted to join in or not. Her perfume caught the back of my throat again and I pulled away as quickly as I could so that the smell wouldn't linger on my clothes for the rest of the day.

'Oh and remind me next time I see you to show you the wedding dress I've chosen. I simply cannot wait for Jack to see me in it. He's just going to adore me even more. I think you and I could be the best of friends you know, Nellie. Wouldn't that be fabulous? Oh my God! Perhaps you could be one of my bridesmaids. Well, maid of honour, you are way too old to be a bridesmaid.' She tittered at her own joke. 'We'd have to get you on a diet, *obvs*. We've got plenty of time though. And we could do with getting you off to the hairdresser's and get this mousy-brown hair of yours sorted out.' She wrapped her fingers around my hair and tugged it slightly.

I winced.

'I'm sure they'll be able to do something nice with the colour and maybe make it more of a style instead of it just hanging there.' She looked me up and down. 'Yes, I'm sure there's so much more we could do with, err...' She circled her finger in the air and then pointed at my body. 'This. And your wardrobe too. You look like you're going to a funeral in what you're wearing today. Oh wait. You are.' She giggled. 'You should wear that on

Monday. It'll be perfect. But your clothes are really something we'll have to work on. Jack is absolutely right. You really are a plain thing, aren't you? I can't wait to get my hands on you. Some fake tan and false eyelashes will make a huge difference for starters. Oh it'll be fabulous. You can be my little project.' She clapped her hands together. 'How very exciting. I can't wait to get started with you.'

I had intended asking her advice about the swishing event I wanted to put together, but I was determined that after that day, I wouldn't lower myself to ask her. I felt so sad. I had been thinking how nice it would be to have a female friend around here and how we both had Jack in common. It really sounded like Jack didn't have the time of day for me any more. That was obviously why he had been quiet with me on the way home from the social evening. Oh well. At least that would sort out my little crush on him reasonably quickly.

'I'm so glad we had this little chat to clear the air,' Natalia went on. 'I think it needed doing. I know you wouldn't want Jack to feel sorry for you and feel like he has to hang around with you all the time, just because you were once the girl who used to "follow him around all the time like a little lap dog" I think his exact words were.'

Could she make me feel any worse? I didn't think so.

'And remember, not a word to a soul. This is our little secret. I've so enjoyed our lunch today and the time we've spent together, Nellie. We must do it again soon.'

Not bloody likely! I managed a weak smile and walked as quickly as I possibly could without tripping over towards the door as I heard her yelling behind me, in that shrill, annoying voice, that she'd call me very soon. I'd managed to keep the tears away until I'd left the table but as I walked towards the door there were tears streaming down my cheeks and I just hoped I could make it to my car before I fell into a crumpled heap. I was so hurt that Jack had said those things to her. I couldn't believe that my Jack, –well, Natalia's Jack now – the Jack who I'd thought was my best friend, who I'd been so happy to see after all these years, could be so cruel. I thought he had been happy to see me, but it turned out I didn't know him at all any more. He clearly wasn't the man I'd thought he was and clearly wasn't the kind, gentle, lovely boy he used to be. You really do live and learn.

Once I'd calmed down enough to open the car's roof and start the drive back to Aunty Lil's, I mulled over all the things Natalia had said while the wind rushed through my hair. I needed the fresh air to clear my head and blow those cobwebs and nasty words away. I realised Jack must have felt obliged to be nice to me when I'd arrived because I didn't know anyone. I banged the side of my clenched first on the steering wheel. I was such a bloody fool.

What had happened with Natalia made me want to go back home to Staffordshire. I needed a hug from my best mate and maybe even her mum.

When I pulled up onto the drive, a lightbulb went off in my head. I sent Shivani a short text asking what time she'd be free later. I'd had a moment of clarity and had made a decision which I really needed to talk through with her.

Chapter Twenty-Two

'LILIAN'S HERE.' DOM came and put his hand on my shoulder.

From the lounge window I could see that the hearse had arrived, with a limo following behind. I took a deep breath.

'Are you OK? Ready to go?' asked Dom. 'You can take as much time as you like if you need a little longer.'

'No, I'm ready. Let's go.'

It had been a strange morning. People had gathered at the house for coffee and cake before heading off to the crem. Miraculously, I'd been able to avoid Jack not only that morning but for most of the weekend too, by only going out to take Norman for a walk when Jack's car wasn't parked next door. He'd been hovering around me but every time he came too near I managed to find someone else to talk to. I couldn't bring myself to speak to him. Not today. I was already teetering on the edge of tears. If anyone said the wrong thing I was pretty sure my emotions would get the better of me.

I'd asked Dom to join me in the front row of the limo, with Jack and his parents on the seat behind. I could feel Jack's eyes boring into the back of my head but I was determined not to turn round to look at him. Val rested her hand on my shoulder, which was a huge comfort.

I didn't really know how to behave today. It had been years since I'd seen Aunty Lil, and the woman I remembered was different to the one many of those attending, who had been her friends in her more recent years, knew. The celebrant had popped round at the weekend to ask if I wanted to say a few words, but I felt a bit of a fraud saying something – also at being upset – when I hadn't made much of an effort to stay in touch with her. I was still so annoyed with myself for letting life get in the way and pass me by without making an effort to repair the rift. I hated the thought that she went to her death, with us not being in touch. I should have done something about it as I became an adult, and definitely once Mum was no longer around. My shoulders felt weighed down with guilt and, more than that, I didn't want people to think badly of me.

Dom squeezed my hand. He really had been so

wonderful throughout this whole process and I honestly didn't know how I would have coped without him.

The car started to travel down the road, slowly at first, with William the funeral director walking in front, until we reached the end of Aunty Lil's street, where he got into the hearse with the driver and the procession to the crem began. As we arrived under the archway outside of the main doors of the crematorium, and William came to open the limo doors, the sun came out from behind the clouds and bathed everyone in sunshine. At the same time, a gaggle of geese flew over in perfect formation.

William winked at me and smiled. 'And there's the fly-by I arranged for Lilian. Don't dwell on the past, my dear. The sunshine shows she's happy that you're here now.'

A lump stuck in my throat. 'You think?' I softly asked, raising my eyebrows.

'I don't think. I know. I've done this before remember.'

I smiled. What a lovely thought and what a kind man to say such a beautiful thing at a very emotional time.

'Ready?' he asked.

I took a huge breath through my nose, held it

for the count of four, slowly exhaled and nodded.

He led us into the small room, following the pall bearers, who placed the coffin on a plinth at the front. The celebrant read out a couple of poems and some funny stories that Aunty Lil's friends had shared and talked about how much she'd done in the community over the years, particularly for the local animal shelter. While it was a sad occasion, it was also joyful to celebrate her life. A life that was evidently full of friendship, love and happiness, judging by the number of people who were there.

As I looked over my shoulder I came eye to eye with Jack. I swiftly averted my gaze and scanned the rest of the room. As we said our final goodbyes to Lilian Eugenie Wagstaff, the curtains closed around the coffin to the sound of 'Somewhere Over the Rainbow', which is a song I chose because she used to sing it to me when I was a girl. I then made my way outside, where I was to meet and greet everyone who had come.

I shook hands with so many people that I'd never even heard of, with them offering their condolences to me, when I felt as if I was the one who should be offering mine to them. Dom, bless him, never left my side and was there to introduce those people he knew, which was almost everyone.

I was on the verge of tears the whole time and willed myself to stay strong.

At the pub, Mary and Bill were waiting at the doors as the cars pulled up. As we walked to the doorway, Mary shouted in a loud voice, 'Welcome to the Cock.' I couldn't help but look at Jack and his eyes were sparkling and I could see the corners of his mouth curling up. He winked and mouthed 'nice cock' to me and I held back an urge to laugh, covering it with a cough instead.

Once the formalities of the service were over, the atmosphere was a little more relaxed and it was lovely to meet Aunty Lil's friends properly and hear stories about her later years that I knew nothing about. Her Pilates teacher told me about the time she first met Lil and was right at the front of the class when she did a huge stretch and farted really loudly. Apparently Aunty Lil just giggled and carried on as if nothing had happened while the whole class fell about laughing.

Pamela from the pet shop told me how they used to go on dog walks together. Apparently Aunty Lil would shout at mountain bikers and one time when someone had appeared right behind them on a bike and just drove through the middle of them both, scaring the dogs, Aunty Lil had yelled, 'Use your fucking bell, you tossing arsehole.' Pamela said that it was so out of character, and that Aunty Lil had actually surprised herself, that they fell about laughing for the rest of the walk.

The sound of a spoon dinging on a glass made everyone turn towards the noise. One of Aunty Lil's bowling crowd was standing on a chair.

'Could I have your attention, please. I hope you don't mind, Nell, but I'd like to say a few words.' He wobbled and steadied himself.

Christ. I really hoped he didn't fall off. Leonard must have been at least ninety years old and I couldn't even begin to think about how the hell he got up there, let alone how he was going to get down, without an army of help. I could see the headlines in the local paper: 'Ninety-year-old dies tragically giving eulogy'.

Leonard said, 'Lilian was a dear friend to all of us here today and we all have so many happy memories of her. So many to talk about for years to come. She was kind and generous, warm-hearted, and always there for us all, and I know I was proud to call her my friend. I'd like you all to join me in raising a glass to dear Lilian Wagstaff.'

'Lilian Wagstaff!' Her name echoed around the room as everyone toasted her.

'I know how much she loved young Nell here

and I'd like to invite Nell to join me in saying a few words too.'

Oh fuck. My heart began to pound. I really wasn't prepared for that. Panic kicked in and my natural instinct was to seek out Jack in the room. Our eyes met across the heads and he swiftly came across to me.

I could feel his warm breath on my neck and it made me shiver as he leant in and whispered, 'You've got this, Nellie-bum! You can do it. Just breathe.' He took my hand and helped me up onto the chair next to Leonard.

'Err, thank you, Leonard. I wasn't expecting to say anything today, so forgive me for being unprepared. As some of you know, I hadn't been in touch with Aunty Lil for a number of years and it really is the one true regret of my life that I didn't get the chance to correct that. I hope she'd forgive me.' I looked upwards and started to well up.

I looked over at Jack and remembered what he'd said – breathe. He winked at me and my heart skipped. He'd always been there for me. Lifting and supporting me. He'd believed in me when I was a girl, when I didn't believe in myself. He grinned. I could do this.

'I just want to thank you all for coming along

today. It really has been wonderful to chat to you all and find out more about Lilian's life and I'd like you all once again to raise your glasses to Aunty Lil.'

Once more an echo of Lil, Aunty Lil and Lilian could be heard and it was so nice that they were all here celebrating her life. I vowed to never waste time again or spend time saying I wish I'd done something. Time was something that you can never get back and life was too short for regrets. I was going to make time for many more things in my life and make wonderful memories along the way.

Natalia came up to where we Jack and I stood and linked her arm through Jack's, smiling sweetly at me. I seemed to be the only one who noticed that it wasn't genuine.

I would be friends with Jack but I would never again let a man hurt me. Not the way that Callum had hurt me by leaving, when he knew that my past was a sore subject for me, or by my dad wanting nothing to do with me, and not by the words that Jack had said about me via Natalia. It was just me now. I was an orphan. I was going to look after myself and be kind to myself. And I was going to make damn sure that I was not going to live the rest of my life full of regret. I was going to do Aunty Lil proud.

Jack offered to come back to the house with me but I didn't want him there. I needed to be alone with my thoughts and my memories on that very poignant day. I didn't want anyone there to try to persuade me from doing what I was going to do next.

For the second time in my life, I drove away from Larkspur Lane in the middle of the night. This time though, there were two letters that I had to post through doors before I went.

One was to Dom to thank him for everything he had done for me and for being a wonderful friend to Lilian and to me. I told him I'd be in touch to sort out arrangements for the sale of the house and the beach hut.

The other was to Jack, to say that I thought we could have been friends in our adult life and that things would maybe pick up where we left off, but that too much had happened over the years. I said that I was sorry if I had made him feel uncomfortable in any way since I'd been back. I thanked him for his friendship and wished him and Natalia health and happiness for their future together.

I turned to look at the house, half expecting Aunty Lil to be waving from one of the windows. She wasn't.

'Come on, Norman. Jump in. Back to reality now and a different life. It's time to go home.'

Chapter Twenty-Three

I T WAS AROUND 2.30 a.m. when we arrived back in Staffordshire. The streets were deserted and it had started to drizzle on the drive back. I couldn't find a parking space anywhere near the house, which was really annoying when I had a carful of stuff. I didn't know whether to leave it all in the car till morning and risk it getting stolen, or unpack in the dark and rain. I dithered.

I wasn't sure how I felt being back. Looking up at that same shiny red front door that not so long ago I was so happy to walk through, felt wrong somehow. It felt unfamiliar, as if I was walking into someone else's house.

'Come on, Norman,' I whispered, aware that everyone in the street around us were sleeping. 'Let's go and see your new home.'

There was post jammed behind the front door which made it awkward to get in, but once we did I shut the door behind us and opened up all the doors off the hall. It smelt musty and would need the windows flung open in the morning to get some fresh air in. Opening up the back door and walking out into the small back yard, which I'd tried to make pretty, I realised that there wasn't an awful lot of room for a dog. It would have to do for him having a wee but then I supposed I'd have to take him to the local park once it was light.

Tiredness swept over me and I called Norman in and went up to bed. The car would have to wait until tomorrow; I was shattered after that long drive. The one thing that I'd brought in from the car was Norman's bed, so I placed it in the hall and when he lay on it, I stroked his head, said goodnight to him and climbed the stairs. Fully clothed I fell into bed, exhausted. What a day.

Whimpering woke me. It was still dark. I looked at the bedside clock and it said 4.30. I'd been asleep less than a couple of hours. Oh man! I could hardly see straight. I looked down and Norman was sitting by the side of me, looking upset. Poor soul. I knew he was only a dog, but he'd been through a lot in the last few weeks and now I'd taken him away from his home and brought him somewhere new. I patted the bed by the side of me and he immediately jumped up and snuggled in. He was shivering, so I covered him with the blanket that lay across the bottom of the bed. He put his paw on my arm and closed his eyes. This was the most physical he'd really been since I'd known him. Progress indeed. Whatever happened, I had Norman.

'Good boy, Normie. I've got you. We're in this together now, mate. Night sweetheart.' I stroked his velvety ears and heard a big sigh escape his sweet little body. We both fell fast asleep.

'Ew! What the…'. A sandpaper-like tongue licking my face woke me and I looked up into big brown eyes staring at me from above. His paws were kneading my tummy. 'Good morning, Norman, what a delightful way to wake up. Thank you.'

He jumped off the bed and ran to the door. Grabbing my robe from the bottom of the bed, I stumbled down the stairs, nearly falling over him as he rushed past. By the time I got there, he was excitedly dancing on all paws by the back door. I let him out, popped on the kettle and checked my phone. It was 9.30. I couldn't believe I'd slept so late.

I had four missed calls from Jack and one from Dom. I also had two voicemails. One from each of them. I immediately deleted Jack's. I needed to move on from him and there was nothing that he could say that would mend things between us.

Natalia had said everything that needed to be said when we met up.

Dom's message though made me smile.

Good morning, Nell. I got your note, thank you for updating me. I was sad to hear that you've decided to go back to the Midlands but understand you need some time away. You have all the time in the world to make your decisions and whatever you choose to do must be right for you. I wish you well. I'm here if I can help. It's been lovely getting to know you over the last few days and I hope that we will remain friends. Keep in touch and good luck with everything.

I really did like him. He was one of the good ones. Typically though, not available to me. But I was glad that he had someone in his life that made him happy. That's all anyone really wants in life. It didn't seem too much to ask for.

Norman trundled back inside and I took my coffee and headed back upstairs to take a shower. Hopefully that might wake me up a little more. As I walked into the bedroom I thought about how my life had changed since the last time I was in that room. I left, heading to Dorset not knowing why. I had no job and no fiancé. But now, I think I might even be a millionaire. And I had a dog.

Norman came in and jumped on the bed, and as I moved across to stroke him, he put his paw up on my shoulder in a protective manner.

'We're going to be OK, Norman. Whatever happens, we're going to be OK.'

He circled round three times and lay down and closed his eyes. No wonder they say it's a dog's life.

A hammering on the door indicated that Shivani had arrived. I ran down the stairs to the front door and flung it open, not even letting her get through it before embracing her.

'Alright bird! So you've missed me. Who wouldn't?' she asked, grinning widely. 'But get the fuck off me, you weirdo.'

Oh how I'd missed her bonkers sense of humour.

She was laden down with a shopping bag on each side. 'So I've brought milk, croissants, jam, bread, but the most important thing of all – cake.' She laid them all out on the tiny kitchen table. God I've missed you, Nell. Get the kettle on and crack open the cake, I'm bloody starving.'

She was one of those people who swept into your house like a whirlwind, left a trail of destruction behind her and then left, with peace and quiet reigning again. And I wouldn't have her any other way.

'Oh how I've missed you too.' It was so good to see her. 'You can't have cake for breakfast, by the way.'

'Who said? I'm an adult, which means I can have what I want for breakfast, actually.'

We both laughed. I hadn't realised just how much I'd missed her while I was away.

I pottered around in the kitchen getting out plates and mugs, trying hard to remember where everything was. This house seemed so unfamiliar to me right now, as if I was staying in someone else's house. It was bizarre when I'd lived there for three years and I hadn't been away that long. I thought back to Aunty Lil's gorgeous, spacious kitchen which overlooked the landscaped back garden and had a pang of longing and squeezed my eyes shut. How ridiculous that the house in Muddleford seemed more like home than this one did. It must have been because I'd been away. Give me a few days at home and I'd be as right as rain.

Norman hovered by the back door again so I let him out. The small back yard was rubbish after what he was used to. He could run around Aunty Lil's garden all day. It would take him seconds to walk the perimeter of this space. I would definitely take him to the park later to make up for it, even though I didn't think I'd ever been to my local park in all the time I'd lived there.

'So come on then, bird. Give me all the goss.'

I loved Shivani's easy manner. She was such fabulous company to be in. I updated her on everything that had happened since I'd been away.

She was much more considered than me when she'd heard it all.

'I don't suppose you've thought that Natalia could have been lying, have you?'

To be honest, that hadn't occurred to me. As someone who rarely even told a white lie, I presumed that everyone was the same.

'She could perhaps just be jealous and staking her claim. You said that Jack had been lovely to you. Surely you can't fake that? Are you sure you haven't acted too rashly by packing up and coming home?'

I loved that she was so open and honest with me. There was no second guessing what she thought. She just came right out with it. It was refreshing and one of the many reasons why I loved being friends with her.

'I know you love it down there, Nell. You light up when you talk about it. You light up when you talk about *him*. You can't hide it. But even if you take him out of the equation, do you think being back here is right for you?'

I honestly did not know the answer.

Three cups of coffee and even more cake later, I was still none the wiser as to whether I'd made the right choice, even though we'd talked through the pros and cons of being in Staffordshire as opposed to being in Dorset. I know I felt something had been missing from my life and I hadn't felt that when I'd been in Muddleford. But that might have been because there were nice things to do down there and back home I literally had nothing to do. If I stayed I needed to find something to fill my days.

As if on cue, Norman came up and shoved a soggy, smelly, furry object on my lap. I'm not sure what cuddly toy it had been originally but he clearly wanted me to play.

'Come on boy.'

After a few minutes of throwing the toy and him running off like a loon to retrieve it, with lots of mock growling and Shivani laughing at us, I glanced at my watch and realised it was nearly lunchtime and I still hadn't taken Norman out for a walk. I was a terrible dog mother.

'Fancy a walk, Shiv? I need to take this little fella out.'

'I love that you have a dog. You seem really contented with each other too. It's fab.'

'To be honest, I was horrified at first when I found out Norman was a dog and not Aunty Lil's boyfriend, but I reckon we muddle along alright together, don't we, my little matey?' I'd never thought I'd be one of those people who spoke to their dogs in silly voices but it turned out I was.

'I'd love to come for a walk but I'm just too glamourous to get all hot and sweaty. Also, I have to go and see Mum this afternoon, but let's have a day together at the weekend. We could go into Birmingham. Have a few cocktails and a bit of lunch. Celebrate your recent good fortune. Fancy it?'

It sounded delightful and we made arrangements. Even though it was a few days away, it was nice to have something to look forward to.

Before she left, Shivani said, 'I hope you and Norman will be very happy with each other. Perhaps you don't need a man in your life after all, just a dog.'

Maybe she was right.

Chapter Twenty-Four

THE LOCAL PARK was amazing. I'd never been before and didn't even know that there was a lake in the middle of it with ducks. Being somewhere different, I was quite apprehensive about letting Norman off the lead, but I'd loaded up my pockets with his favourite treats and hoped for the best.

He was really well behaved till he found the ducks and launched himself into the lake.

So, dogs don't come with a handbook, or I'd have looked for the page that tells you if you should jump in after them or just let them come out when their fun is over. I remembered Jack's words about making it fun for them to come back to you, so I spent at least ten minutes feeling like a complete tit, shouting, 'Come on Normie, let's go!' in a high-pitched voice, which got gradually deeper and sounded more pissed off as the minutes rolled by and he ignored me completely. He was having the time of his life until the ducks flew off and he was left alone. When he eventually graced me with his presence, he looked half the size he had been when he went in and was dripping everywhere. He then shook all the drips over me.

'Ew, you little bugger.'

He just panted and doggy grinned. A slight breeze wafted by.

'God, you stink, mister.'

I made him come to heel and we walked away from the water and more into the main park itself. We were walking across the disused bowling green when a pretty little blonde cocker spaniel appeared from nowhere. She scampered around Norman and then turned and thrust her rear end at him. He clearly thought he was in for a bit of 'how's your father' and hopped right on. 'Poppy', as I discovered the other dog was called from the owner's screeching with flailing arms, seemed to be having a lovely time and judging from Norman's doggy grin, so was he.

After separating them, to Norman's disgust, Poppy's owner and I ended up having a raging slanging match where she ended with, 'If you can't control your feral mutt, you should keep it on a bloody lead.'

Deeply offended that she'd called Norman a mutt, I took him by the collar, attached his lead and yelled, 'Perhaps if you didn't allow your floozy of a dog to stick her arse in the air like a little doggy slut, then it wouldn't be a problem.'

At that point I stuck my nose in the air and huffed off in the opposite direction but not before shouting over my shoulder, 'Anyway! Norman can't help it if he's a fanny magnet for the local bitches,' to the horror of a little grey-haired old lady who was walking past. I nodded at her as she stared at me, realising how ridiculous I must have sounded but I wasn't prepared to back down one little bit.

I giggled to myself when I stopped to sit on a bench at the entrance to the park before heading home, seeing the funny side of the altercation, now I wasn't stuck in the middle of the first doggy shag I'd ever experienced.

Oh I couldn't wait to tell Jack, he'd it hilarious. But there it was. Jack wasn't mine to tell. I'd moved back. Jack wasn't in my life anymore and I couldn't really break my promise to myself not to contact him on my first day. I couldn't lie, not even to myself. He'd only been back in my life for a short time, but I already really missed him. I missed the way he threw his head back and how his dimple twitched and his face lit up when he laughed. I missed his funny quips, and the constant shoulder barges into me. I missed the way I felt when he was around me – safe and always smiling. I missed him calling me Nellie-bum. The only person in the world who called me that, even now after all those years. I missed everything about him and I felt it deep within the pit of my stomach.

What if I'd made a mistake and Shivani was right and Natalia was lying? What if, even if she Natalia was telling the truth, Jack and I could start all over again and still be the best of friends and I'd get over my romantic feelings towards him? What if having Jack in my life as a friend, was better than not having Jack in my life at all?

I remembered years ago when I talked to Aunty Lil about Mum and Dad splitting up, and I asked what if I could make them love each other again. Her words came back to me now.

'Nell, my darling. Life can be full of what-ifs and should-haves if we let it be. But they'll eat you up inside. Worry about the things that you can do something about, and not the things that you can't.'

I couldn't stop thinking about those words on the walk home. As we passed the Merc parked a good way down the road from the house, I remembered that there were still quite a few boxes that needed taking in. Callum had had a car, and used to moan that he couldn't get a space outside his own front door but when we viewed the house, it was all we could really afford. It was annoying not being able to park on a drive, which I'd got used to doing down in Dorset. I realised that now I had some money, I didn't need to be in this house. I could be anywhere. Perhaps thinking about that could be a little project over the next few days.

Norman ponged!

'Sorry, mate, but you are going to have a shower. Where's Pamela when you need her, eh?'

He slunk off onto his bed before I could stop him. Great, now that would need washing too! I enticed him up the stairs with a salmon treat; his favourite. Everything to do with dogs was smelly I'd noticed. The smellier things were, the more the dog liked them. Bizarre.

I grabbed him by his collar before he launched himself onto my bed.

'Oh no you don't!' Come on!'

The shower wasn't really big enough for one person, let alone a person *and* a dog, but by the time we'd used the entire contents of my Jo Malone English Pear and Freesia body and hand soap, he was definitely smelling much better, even if the bathroom looked like a tornado had been through it. Water soaked the floor, there were soap suds all up the walls and he'd then escaped the bathroom and run around the bedroom with his wet feet. Thank God I'd thought to shut the bedroom door. At this point I was drenched from head to toe, so thought it easiest to have a shower myself. I plonked him on the bed on top of a pile of towels. At least I could throw the lot in the washer when I was done.

When I got out of the shower, and was drying myself, Norman started barking at the bedroom door. Wrapped in just a towel, I went to the door and slowly opened it. He wiggled his way through my knees and I screamed. There was someone stood in front of me and Norman had launched himself at the intruder and knocked him to the floor nearly toppling him down the stairs. Norman was making a deep continuous growl and baring his teeth.

'What the fuck, Nell?'

'Callum, what the hell are you doing here? I seem to remember you'd moved out.' I clung to the towel. As if he hadn't humiliated me enough, all I needed was for that to come undone and me flash my fandango at him.

'Well it's still half my house at the moment, so I'll come and go as I please. Anyway, what are *you* doing here?' He struggled to get up and kicked out at Norman, who started barking aggressively. Callum pressed himself against the landing wall. 'And call the mutt off, for fuck's sake!'

'I think you'd better go downstairs and I'll get dressed and be down in a few minutes. Norman, come here, boy.' I patted him on the head. 'Good boy.'

'Good fucking boy? He nearly had my leg off.'

'I'm sure if he'd have wanted to, he would've. Now please go downstairs.'

I pressed my back against the bedroom door and waited for my heartbeat to slow down. He had scared the living daylights out of me. I was so glad Norman had been here to warn me that something was going on. I was intrigued to know what the hell Callum was doing in my house. Our house, I supposed. I threw on a pair of jogging bottoms and a vest top and scraped my hair back into a pony-tail. This outfit definitely didn't bring me joy, but right now I didn't really care what I looked like. Callum had already dumped me once, so it wasn't like I was trying to make a good impression on him.

BY THE TIME I got downstairs Callum had made himself comfortable with a cup of coffee and *my*

packet of biscuits. Cheeky git.

'Make yourself at home why don't you?'

'Thanks. I did.' He seemed to miss my sarcasm. 'You're looking good, Nell. Got a bit of colour on you. It suits you.'

'What are you doing here, Callum? You left, remember?'

'I did and I realised that I made a huge mistake, Nell. It's not what I want. I want you. I've decided.'

Well I wasn't expecting that!

'Why do you want me, Callum?'

'We go together, like strawberries and cream. Like salt and pepper. Like Kanye and Kim.' His last choice of pairing made me laugh as I was sure they were in the process of splitting up.

'But you left, Callum.'

'But now I'm back.' He smiled and patted the seat beside me. 'I want us to go back to where we were. I just got cold feet. Pre-wedding jitters. This is where I belong. I do have to ask though, why are you looking after a dog?'

Norman hadn't moved from my side while Callum had been speaking. Callum moved to reach out to him and Norman growled. Callum retracted his hand pretty quickly.

'I'm going to make a drink. I presume you

didn't make me one?' I looked at his mug on the table.

'No, sorry. I never thought, but if you're making one, I could manage another, thanks.' He held his cup up and smiled.

I went to take it from him but then remembered what he'd put me through and pulled away walking out of the room. I stood in the kitchen, which before we'd been to the park, was immaculate. Now, there were tea stains all over the counter, a spent teabag left on the side of the sink, the milk hadn't been put back in the fridge and the cupboard door where the cups were kept, was half open. I'd forgotten what a messy person Callum was in the kitchen. He insisted on everywhere else being perfect but the kitchen in his eyes was my domain.

I realised I still hadn't answered his question about the dog, but also that I didn't actually owe him an explanation anyway. Old habits were hard to break. But just what the hell did he think he was playing at? And more than that, what on earth was I meant to do?

Chapter Twenty-Five

COME ON, NELLIE. You've got this. After a deep breath, I took my cup of tea through to the lounge and sat in the armchair opposite Callum, observing him over the top of my cup as I sipped at the drink. I wasn't going to admit that it was roasting hot and burning my tongue. I needed to show him my cool, calm exterior and let him do the talking. He didn't comment that I hadn't made him one.

'So I was thinking I could grab all my stuff from Pete's, where I've been staying, and move back in this afternoon. We could have a Chinese and a bottle of wine tonight to celebrate and maybe have a little snuggle up on the sofa and see what comes up.' He winked at me and grinned.

I used to love that face. I really did. It was amazing how much you can love someone one minute and the next your feelings have changed so dramatically. Hurt can do that to you.

I couldn't believe that just a short time ago I

was going to marry this man. He'd meant the world to me. But then he'd thought nothing of hurting me so much by going behind my back with someone else and then leaving me to be with her. Yet right now he thought he could walk back into my life, just as easily as he'd walked out.

'After all,' he went on. 'I don't suppose you've got round to finding a lodger, taking my name off the rental documents or rented something else yet. Admin never really was your strong point was it? My darling.' Those two words were a complete afterthought and he smiled sweetly.

I wanted to slap his face. Cheeky bastard. Had I really been planning to spend the rest of my life with him? What was I thinking? Or was I just still annoyed with him? God it was hard to work through your emotions when they were all over the place. I felt like I was on a real rollercoaster and didn't know how to get off.

'Come on, babe. We were so good together. Weren't we?'

I thought back to the day I came home and found him leaving me. He didn't say we were good together then. He said that we were mismatched and wanted different things in life. He'd clearly wanted someone different which is why he'd been off shagging Saskia behind my back.

He stood and walked over to me and perched on the arm of my chair, draping his arm around my shoulders. My skin felt like a million ants were crawling all over it. He tickled the back of my neck, I think mistaking my shiver for ecstasy. All I could think of right now was smacking his hand away in anger. I didn't want him touching me.

I eased myself away from him and stood over him. How dare he think he can just wander back in here when it suited him.

'No!'

'Sorry. What do you mean "no"? Would you rather we have Indian instead of Chinese?'

'It's not the food, Callum. It's you. You hurt me. You left me with no warning. You told me you didn't want to marry me any more. You said you didn't love me.'

'Yeah, I know, but I didn't mean it. Like I said, it was just cold feet. I've got it all out of my system now and I know it's you I want.'

'But perhaps now I don't want you.'

He laughed. 'But you love me, Nell. You didn't want me to leave. You said so. You begged me to stay.'

'But despite all that you still left, Callum.'

'And now I'm back.'

I moved across to the settee that he'd vacated. I

just couldn't sit near him right now. It was all too confusing.

'What about Saskia?'

'What *about* Saskia? She couldn't match up to you. I missed you every day. She was just a diversion. I came to my senses. She meant nothing to me. I really do mean that, Nell. You have to believe me.'

'And now you think it's OK to just come walking back in here and pick up where you left off? Is that what you think happens in a situation like this?'

'I know you're pissed with me, Nell, but we can get through this. We really can. Please just give me a chance. Let me make it up to you.' He looked at me and fluttered his long lashes.

I used to love those eyes. Did I still? An image of Jack flashed into my mind. My gorgeous Jack. I felt a stabbing pain in my stomach. Jack didn't want me. He'd let me down. He had Natalia. There was no chance for us and I had to accept that.

I'd spent all my life trying to work out what more I could do to make people love me, to work out what I'd done wrong. Why didn't Mum love me enough to stop drinking? Why did Dad walk out of our lives and never come back? Even Aunty

Lil became a distant memory. And then, to top the lot, good-hearted, kind and wonderful Jack didn't want me. What did I have to change to be the person they needed me to be so they would love me?

Yet here was Callum, offering me a life with him again.

When I met Callum, I believed he did truly love me. We fitted together and muddled along well. It worked. When we discussed marriage, it might not have been the big romantic proposal I'd dreamt of since I was a little girl, more of a 'suppose we should get married' type of statement, but I thought that it was OK and that we'd be together forever. I felt that finally I belonged somewhere. I'm not saying it was perfect. Far from it, as I'd realised having been thinking back for the last few days. And then he left me too.

However, right now, he was the only one here. And the only one with anything to offer. Wouldn't being with someone be better than being alone? Did I give us another chance? Could we make it work again? Could I forgive what he'd done to me? So many questions spinning inside my head.

He could tell that I was wavering.

'We don't have to go ahead with the wedding plans. Just put everything on hold.'

'Most of the things have been cancelled anyway.'

'Well there you go then. We won't have that pressure hanging over us any more.'

Getting married shouldn't feel like a pressure, surely. Shouldn't it feel like the best feeling in the world? You were going to marry your soul mate and vow to each other to be together forever. Not just until the next Saskia came along. I couldn't seem to get that out of my head. It felt like it was going to explode.

'I don't have a job any more.'

'We can sort everything out, babe. You and me. What do you say?'

He clearly didn't know about my recent windfall. I was glad. As far as I was aware, only Shivani and her family knew. There shouldn't be any other way that he would have found out. If we did try again, I wanted to make sure it was because he wanted *me*.

'Now that we don't have the wedding going ahead, we don't have to be saving money and we can go and do fun things together.'

'What sort of things, Callum? What things do you want to do now, that you didn't want to do with me before? You used to say that we were two people in a relationship and living in a house, but that we didn't need to be "joined at the hip" I think your actual words were. Why all of a sudden do you want us to do things together? What do you think we didn't do before, that could make everything better now?'

'We could go out to bars, nightclubs, have fun.'

Did he know me at all? Going to a loud bar or a club, with booming music so loud you can't hear yourself speak, was my worst nightmare. Not my thing at all. I pulled a face.

'Maybe go out for more meals together. We spent so long saving up for the wedding, we rarely went out to eat.'

Now that I could cope with. A nice restaurant from time to time would be good.

'I could get you trying out some extreme sports, maybe go on an action holiday together. In fact, did you even cancel the honeymoon? Perhaps we could still go.' His little face lit up.

'I cancelled it. We had to cancel by a certain time so we didn't have to pay it in full. You told me you didn't want to go. Remember? When I suggested we still go to Barbados, you told me you didn't love me any more.' That little nugget of hurt had clearly slipped his mind.

'I'm sorry, Nell. I truly am. Let me make it up to you. Please? I love you. Don't throw it all away.'

Did he mean it? Should I trust him again?

'But I'm not the one who would be throwing it all away, Callum. You already did.'

'I know and I'm a fool. But you loved me. Didn't you? We were good together, weren't we?' He ran his finger down my cheek. 'I've missed you.'

All of a sudden, the room started to spin, and I felt light-headed. I needed some air.

'I need a minute!' I rushed out of the room and made my way to the downstairs loo, where I took some deep breaths and I felt a little less panicked. This was just all too much for me right now. It was blowing my mind!

I grabbed a cardigan from the bottom of the stairs. It was one of Aunty Lil's that I'd brought with me. For an old lady, she wore some pretty fabulous clothes. I wrapped it around my shoulders and shivered. I felt cloaked in warmth and love and shoved my hands in the pockets for extra comfort. I felt something beneath my fingers and there was a small piece of card. On it there was a beautiful picture of colourful flowers and the words: 'It's better to regret something you've done, than not try in the first place.' Very apt for the moment. Was it a sign? Oh, Nell, don't be ridiculous. I twirled the card around in my fingers and noticed a message on the other side too which said, 'Trust your instincts.'

I opened the back door and breathed in the fresh air but left it open. The house felt stifling.

I heard the low vibration of a voice from the lounge. The door was slightly ajar, and I could see that Callum was on the phone. His voice was low but I could catch snippets.

I heard him say, 'It's just a matter of time, mate. I'm pretty sure I'll be sleeping here tonight with all my things back in place. Thanks for putting me up, mate. I can't believe that bloody bitch Saskia dumped me.'

I gasped.

'It's all worked out perfectly, to be honest. She's inherited all that money and property and I need somewhere to live. Bingo! And I just have to be nice for a bit and get my feet back under the table before I can start to relax again. Although the dozy mare has cancelled the holiday to Barbados so it doesn't look like I'll be going there after all. Shame! I was looking forward to that and pretty confident she wouldn't have cancelled it so soon. Perhaps she had given up on me after all.' He laughed quietly. 'Cheers, mate. Thanks for everything.'

I tiptoed back into the kitchen so he hadn't

guessed that I'd heard everything and made a big deal of coughing as I walked down the hallway back into the lounge.

Norman appeared by my side and right on cue, as we went into the lounge, before I could say any more, he started to bark. Not at anything in particular, but just to get my attention.

'And what is that bloody mutt doing in my house?'

'This is not your house any more. You left. This is Norman and he's mine. And he's not a mutt.'

'You know I'm allergic to dogs.'

'Well you weren't here.'

'But I'm here now.' He pouted. That was the face he knew used to get him his own way every time. 'You know I never wanted a dog.'

'Like I said, you weren't here. You left me. Remember?'

'I'm back though now, Nell, and I think you need to make a choice. It's the dog or me.'

Chapter Twenty-Six

A COLD, WET nose on my face woke me. I rolled over. A paw on my back, gave me a gentle nudge. I put the pillow over my head. A little whine was the last straw.

'OK, OK I'm getting up.'

I grabbed the robe from the bottom of my bed and glanced out the window. The weather looked grey and drizzly. I missed the sunshine. And the sea air. Every day that I'd woken up in Muddleford, the sun had shone through my bedroom window and I had got up and opened the balcony windows. Once I'd let Norman out and made a cuppa, we'd take it back up to bed and I'd sit and read for a bit, or sometimes I just gazed out at that amazing view. Seeing the sea filled my soul with joy. I remembered Aunty Lil teaching me a quote by Jacques Cousteau and those words came back to me now. 'The sea, once it casts its spell, holds one in its net of wonder forever.' I felt a pang to be back in Muddleford. Not in drizzly damp Staffordshire.

I opened the back door to let Norman into the yard. He didn't look too keen and I couldn't say I blamed him.

'Go on! Out you go.'

He slunk out and it took him two seconds to have a wee and come back in again. His favourite new pastime was piddling up my stunning lavender bush that I'd been cultivating for the last three years. Earlier this year it came out in its full gorgeous purple glory, the glorious perfume permeating the air as soon as the door was opened. I had been immensely proud of it. Now the majority of it was brown and definitely dead and that was from just a couple of days of wee.

I looked up at the sky. The clouds looked full of rain and I didn't relish going out in it. But that was the thing about having a dog. You had to go out whether you liked it or not. They didn't ask much of you apart from at least one walk a day, some food and clean water, which wasn't much really.

We did go back up to bed, but Norman was restless and the room was dark and didn't feel right.

I knocked on the door of the spare room and received a grunt in return and a shuffling sound getting nearer to the door. Callum appeared in a pair of boxer shorts. He stank of alcohol. It was a smell I hated. Callum used to say I was boring and that I should drink more and loosen up but I wasn't a big drinker. I'd seen the damage it could do to you first-hand. After Mum died, I didn't touch the stuff for years, but then as time went on I did partake in the odd glass, maybe two, but that was my limit on a normal night unless Shivani was in the vicinity and I seemed to throw caution to the wind.

I looked at Callum, his hair stuck up all over the place, and I'd definitely seen him looking better. After I'd confronted him the day before when he came off the phone, he broke down and confessed everything. I actually felt so sorry for him, when he said that he had nowhere else to go, that I said he could stay for a few days in the spare room. There was no way he was getting back into my bed. And he was told in no uncertain terms that Norman was going nowhere.

I hadn't slept well but had come to some very big decisions the night before. Callum promised to keep out of my way as much as possible, and once I'd spoken to Shivani I'd tell him of my plans.

WHEN SHIVANI CAME to the house late on Saturday

morning to pick me up for lunch, she had the surprise of her life when Callum answered the door to her. Fury flooded through her veins as she grabbed me by the elbow and dragged me into the lounge.

'Nell, what the fuck are you thinking about, taking him back after all he's done?'

I held my palm up to her. 'Stop right there. I haven't taken him back. I've just given him somewhere to stay. Do you really think I'm that soft?'

She raised her eyebrows. 'Oh. OK then. Tell me how you got to this point.'

'Come on, let's go out, I don't want to do it here.' I patted Norman on the head and told him to go lie down and Shivani and I walked to the car and I drove us to our favourite local Italian restaurant.

I didn't mind leaving Norman with Callum for a couple of hours. They were tolerating each other, and even though Callum had the constant sneezes around Norman, he spent so much time in the spare room it didn't affect him as much as he had originally thought. To be honest, as I did say to him, he had two choices and certainly could find somewhere else to stay if he wasn't happy.

I filled in Shivani over lunch, telling her about

catching Callum on the phone and him confessing to finding out from Shivani's older brother that I'd come into some money.

'I'll bloody kill Nassir for letting the cat out of the bag.'

'Don't worry, it's all for the best. Apparently he only said it because he was sticking up for me, so it was all done with the best of intentions. Calm down, Shivani. Honestly it's all fine.

'I'm going to tell Callum that he can take over the house, I don't want to be there any more. There's nowhere for Norman and walking in the park with a million other dogs isn't great for him. He's like a different dog up here. He's starting to lunge at other male dogs that come near us, and he tries to shag every female dog he comes into contact with.' Shivani's mouth twitched at this. 'And he needs to run free on the beach. And for that matter, so do I. So, I've made my decision and I'm going to go and live in Muddleford.'

She gasped and held her hand to her chest.

'I know Jack doesn't want to be with me, in that way, but if he and Natalia are getting married then at least he won't be living next door and I'll get over it. I've got a beautiful house there, the beach hut, although it seems a bit surplus to requirements if I've already got a house that overlooks the sea. I can make a new life down there.'

'Your face lights up when you talk about "down there"!' Shivani laughed. 'I'll miss you, you daft cow.' A tear rolled down her cheek.

'I'll miss you too, but it's literally two-and-a-half hours away and instead of snatching lunches and quick drinks after work here, perhaps you'll be able to come and stay for weekends and we can have some proper quality time together. And do you know what? If after six months I'm not loving it, then I can come back. Thanks to Aunty Lil, I now have the funds and the freedom to do what I want. What do you think, Shivani? Am I being irrational?'

'I think it's a really good decision, babe. And you just try and stop me from coming to stay. You'd just better hope I don't bump into Jack or I'll be offering him a piece of my mind and telling him how stupid he is to not be in love with you. You're a catch, babe. If I was a bloke, I'd bag you.'

I laughed. If a boyfriend tried as hard to please you as your best friend did, then relationships would be a whole lot easier. There was something very special about a best-friend relationship. You lift each other. You work together. Another Aunty Lil's sayings popped into my head: 'A rising tide lifts all boats.'

Shivani had inherited some wonderful qualities from her mum, who was a very special lady who helped others all of the time and never put herself first. She felt that by helping others first, you in turn would be helped, if and when you needed it. In turn everyone would benefit. I knew that Shivani and I wouldn't let a little thing like a couple of hundred miles come between us.

Shivani grabbed my hand across the table and squeezed it. 'I really will miss you, though. We all will. I don't want to get too soppy but I think we have a 'once in a lifetime' friendship that some people don't ever have. We're so lucky that we found each other.' She wiped her eyes. 'Mum will love your decision. She said right from the start that you should live down there. She might be coming to visit with me.'

'Now that I can definitely cope with. I'll miss you too, but we wouldn't see each other in the week here anyway now we're not working together. Now you have your new job you'll be busy all the time and we'll make diary dates to get together. We'll make it happen. Just because I'm not round the corner, you're not getting rid of me that easily. You're stuck with me.'

'I think you've made a wonderful decision, hon. I really do.'

It had taken me a couple of days of constant

phone calls to put everything in place. We spoke to the bank and Dom had been an absolute star, getting everything moving really quickly from a legal point of view. We transferred everything in Staffordshire across to Callum's name with immediate effect. He had decided that he'd still like to live in the house, rather than move somewhere else, and agreed to take over the rental agreement and bills. Because I wasn't desperate for money we agreed a nominal amount that I would get for the furniture as I'd bought the majority of it. I wasn't bothered about getting anything, but Dom advised me that just because I'd come into money, it didn't mean that I could throw it away willy-nilly and still deserved to get my share of what I'd put into the house.

We agreed that a new start would be good for us both. This time as we parted company on the doorstep of our house, we were very adult and gave each other a brief hug and wished each other well for the future.

Even though he'd hurt me, I felt like the experience had made me grow and learn. I suppose that's all you can ask from each phase of your life.

Yet another of Aunty Lil's expressions – 'You are the author of your own life. You can make it anything you want it to be' – came to me. I'd never felt closer to her than I had just lately. I believed she was helping to guide me in the right direction. The next chapter of my life held a lot of uncertainty, but for the first time in a very long time I was excited and looking forward to a new adventure, whatever it brought. And, after all, I wasn't alone. I had Norman.

And that's how just a couple of days later, Norman and I drove off, for what would very probably be the last time, from that house in that town and just under three hours later we arrived back in the pretty little village of Muddleford. As we passed the 'Welcome to Muddleford' sign my shoulders relaxed and I breathed a sigh of relief. The late-afternoon sun was still beating down on the windscreen and when I opened the window, the fishy, tangy smell of the sea air hit my nostrils. As I registered the familiar sound of squawking seagulls it was as if all my senses had once again sprung to life. The sound of Norman's tail thumping like mad against the leather back seat as he recognised the sight of his own street was a joy. Pulling up on the drive at Aunty Lil's house, which I really needed to start calling 'my house', felt more right than anything else had ever felt in my life. I let out the biggest sigh.

'Come on Norman. We're home.'

Chapter Twenty-Seven

WAKING UP BACK in Muddleford felt great. The sunlight burst through the curtains and when I flung them open the sight of the cerulean-blue sky put me immediately into a feel-good mood. I'd dropped a text to Val the night before, to say I was back and not to worry if she noticed someone in the house. She had texted back to say welcome home and that she'd see me soon for a coffee and a catch-up. I didn't realise how much I'd missed her and was really looking forward to seeing her.

I jumped out of bed, headed downstairs and popped the coffee machine on, something else I'd missed, and went and sat in the back garden where the salty sea air mixed with the aroma of freshly ground coffee. I wished I could bottle the smell of a Muddleford morning and sell it. I'd make a fortune.

It felt so good to be back but it was something more than good. It felt right. I felt with every essence of my being, that this was where I was meant to be. Whatever happened, hopefully Jack and I could come out of this situation being friends at least. I wished him happiness in his life, and if I couldn't have him, then I wished he was happy with the girl who was lucky enough to have him in her life. And that girl, Natalia, I would also make an effort with and try to be her friend. We'd never be besties, but perhaps we'd be acquaintances. She needed to know that I caused her no harm and was no threat to her and Jack. I would make the effort to find her and tell her that. I was pretty sure that if I did, we could all move on.

Norman danced around my feet, urging me to drink up. I pulled on clean undies, a pair of shorts and a t-shirt, slipped my trainers on at the door and we headed to the beach. Halfway down the steps, I spotted another painted rock. *Peace* was the word that shimmered in silver paint. Every time I saw one, the thought that someone, probably Aunty Lil, had painted these for other people to lift them each time they were spotted made me smile.

The morning sun shone down upon us, I could feel the heat warming my skin. I had to remember to put on suntan lotion when I came out. The heat on this beach had caught me by surprise in the past. A game of throw and fetch left Norman and me both feeling invigorated and after about half an hour, I opened up the beach hut as I needed the loo. The sun hadn't had chance to warm it up just yet but hanging up on a hook on the back of the loo door was another old cardigan. Aunty Lil must have been a bit of a cardigan queen. The thought made me laugh because that's what Callum used to call me. I draped it around my shoulders, then opened a deck chair and sat overlooking the sea while Norman curled up on the rug and had a snooze. Something hard was digging into my side and I dug deep into the pocket of the cardy. Another card was tucked into the bottom corner. I retrieved it and read the message: 'Everything that we do and everyone that we meet is put in our path for a purpose.' Marla Gibbs.

I'd never heard of Marla Gibbs but she sounded like a wise lady. I would look her up when I got home later. Aunty Lil had a noticeboard up on the wall next to the door with criss-cross elastic to hold things in place. It would be the perfect place for this card. I decided to put the other one there too. I felt that this hut was going to be a place that might bring me some inspiration for how to move my life forward.

I was trying to summon up some enthusiasm

and ideas about getting rid of Aunty Lil's clothes, when a voice interrupted my thoughts.

'Morning, dear, you must be Nell.' A tall, dark-haired, attractive lady walked towards me smiling. She must have been in her sixties. 'You're a dead ringer for her, you know, when she was younger. Such a beauty she was. And she never even realised.' I smiled. 'I'm Joan, m'dear.' She leaned towards me and shook my hand. 'We were in the Women's Institute together. We all miss her dreadfully. She was a bright ray of sunshine and a joy to have around. Sadly I wasn't able to make her funeral because my husband was having a hip operation.'

'Aw thank you, Joan. I hope the hip is mending well. Would you like to join me for a coffee?'

'Oh I won't keep you, m'dear. I'm sure you've got enough to be getting on with rather than chatting with a silly old thing like me.'

'I'd love you to join me. It's been wonderful to meet Aunty Lil's friends. I learnt lots about her at the get-together after the funeral, and it would be lovely to hear about her WI adventures too. I hear that you ladies at the WI are a force to be reckoned with.'

'Oh we are. It's not all jam and Jerusalem you know. And only if you are sure. It would be lovely to stop for a break. I've been trying to get my steps in this morning and I've already done just over 8k today. I'm bloody knackered.'

I tittered as I got up and invited her to take my seat, while I pulled another deckchair down from the hook on the wall and flicked on the kettle before joining her. Norman raised his head to see what the commotion was about and then flopped down again.

'You know, you should come along and meet the others. I know not everyone was able to get to the Cock.' I tried not to smirk. 'It would be lovely for you to meet everyone. Unless you are too busy, of course. We have a meeting this week in fact. On Thursday morning. Oh please say you'll come.'

'I'd really love that. I'm really not *that* busy. In fact I'm not busy at all and it would be lovely to come along and meet everyone.'

Joan smiled. 'So, if you don't mind me asking, what are your plans? Do you know? Will you stay here in Muddleford?'

'Definitely for the time being.' If felt really good to say that.

'Obviously you're quite an independent and wealthy young lady now. I hope you don't mind me saying, but we had a lady come to the WI to talk to us about making a will, and Lilian told everyone she was leaving everything to you. Do you even need to work?' She clutched her hand to her chest. 'Oh goodness, I'm sorry. Do forgive me. My husband is always saying I'm a nosy old biddy. It's nothing to do with me.'

'I don't mind at all, Joan. I've nothing to hide. To be honest, I don't know what I'm going to do with myself. All I really have to do is clean the house, shop and walk Norman, so I'll definitely need to find something else to do with my time.'

'Why don't you join us at the WI? You can take over Lilian's membership. She'd love that. She'd be cheering us on from up above.' She looked up at the sky and smiled. 'Just come along on Thursday and meet everyone. Find out all about the charity initiatives we get involved in. We have all sorts of trips out and people coming in to talk to us. We sometimes have a fashion show too. In fact, we have one coming up very soon. And I'd like to point out that you won't be the youngest member there either. Our group range from Lauren, who is just eighteen and comes along with her Mum, up to Val our vice president, who is seventy-seven. Lilian was our oldest member.' She smiled sadly. 'Of course, you know Val, she's your neighbour.'

'Oh brilliant, I'll come along with her then.

She'll have all the details, will she?'

'She most certainly will. She's not missed a meeting in thirty years. It's funny that people think that the WI is for older people, but it really isn't. I think the average age of our group is around forty, so while it's a little older than you, it's definitely not full of old wrinklies like me.' Her giggly laugh was a pleasure to hear. 'We have some wonderful ladies. It will give you the chance to meet them all and maybe make some new friends. And of course hear some more Lilian stories.'

I loved the sound of the WI. I thought it would be a perfect opportunity for what I needed in my life right then. I don't think that you can ever meet enough people along the way. While Shivani would always be my best friend I really did think that meeting other people broadens your horizons and, let's face it, down here in Muddleford, my horizons apart from the one in front of me right now, were pretty narrow.

'There are lots of ladies who live alone and joined originally because they didn't have many friends, and the friendships we've all made over the years, really have been wonderful. Oh look, here's Val now. Her ears must have been burning.'

Val walked towards me with her arms outstretched and wrapped me in a warm heartfelt hug.

I didn't want her to let go. It had been a while since I'd been hugged like that. In fact, it was when I'd first arrived.

'Welcome home, darling. I'm so glad you're back.' She turned to my visitor and beamed. 'Hi, Joan, how are you? I was going to call you when I got back from my walk to say that the woman from the fashion show has cancelled.'

'Oh bugger. That's a real blow. I was really looking forward to that.'

My ears pricked up.

'Fashion show, did you say?'

'Yes, we had a fashion show planned in a couple of weeks' time. It was a fashion show cum jumble sale, really. Lots of pre-owned stuff but only worn once or twice. We were all so looking forward to it.'

'Aha. Well I might be able to help you out there.' Marla Gibbs and her little bit of a kick up the bum seemed to be exactly the thing that was needed. 'Grab a seat, Val, I'll go and make another round of drinks. I've got an idea that might just help us all out of a situation.'

Chapter Twenty-Eight

BY THE TIME I packed the hut up for the day it was nearly 4 o'clock. Joan had been and fetched some snacks from the beach café and we'd drunk gallons between us. Val said it was good experience for the WI meetings because they drank lots of tea and ate a lot of cake. It was sounding more perfect for me by the minute and I was very happy to practise those life skills. I had written lists galore and had lots of jobs to go away and get stuck into. I couldn't wait to get started.

It would do me the world of good to have a project to focus on. I loved where I was and I loved walking on the beach with Norman, and the day I'd spent with Joan and Val had been most enjoyable, but as someone who had got into the habit of getting up every day and going to work, and not had a day off sick in the last eight years, it all felt a bit weird and as if I was at a bit of a loose end. I needed a purpose.

Before I left I had put on a long, pale-lemon

cashmere cardigan I'd noticed on one of the hooks on the hut wall and, as I walked back up the steps, I pulled another card from the right-hand pocket: *Do not fear. Love will find a way.*

It had been quiet around the house since I'd been back. I couldn't lie and say that I hadn't noticed that Jack's missing presence was like a constant ache in my stomach. I hadn't even seen his car for a few days and didn't like to mention it to Val. I had dropped a couple of hints but she'd not picked up on them at all.

It was two days later, when Val and I walked through the doors of the village hall and I had the first of many hot drinks thrust into my hands and one by one I met the Muddleford chapter of the WI. What an absolute delight they were. Joan was president and welcomed everyone to the meeting and introduced me to the group as their very special guest.

'Now we have a little surprise for Nell,' Joan announced.

Oh no! I wasn't a big lover of surprises since I surprised Callum one night by dressing seductively in stockings and suspenders and not an awful lot else, which I knew he liked, and when I shouted surprise as he walked through the lounge door, I was the one who left the room red-faced as well as bare-arsed when most of the rugby team followed him in.

'We've been doing a little bit of homework for you, Nell, and one by one, I'm going to ask each member to come to the front to tell me how they knew Lilian and what they remember the most about her.'

Pamela from the groomers had us all hooting with laughter when she talked about the first time Aunty Lil had gone into the shop and had taken one of the freshly baked biscuits that were on the counter and spat it out when she realised they were made from liver and bacon and weren't for the consumption of people with two legs.

Margaret, who was married to the butcher, Walter, laughed about the fact that Lilian used to spend more money each week on feeding Norman on the best cuts of meat, that most of the times she visited she had to be reminded by Walter to buy something for her own dinner too.

Karen from the hairdresser's next to Pamela's told us about the way Lilian talked about Norman and her spa days, when she'd drop him into the groomer while she popped to the hairdresser and beautician, and both went home looking and smelling beautiful as well as being relaxed and pampered.

Juliette from the local dog rescue shelter talked about the night that Lilian slept on her lounge floor, comforting a dog called Norman, who slept on the sofa, who had been poorly and had been sent back to the shelter from the vet's, who just needed some love and attention after being neglected by a family who didn't have time for him. Lilian fostered Norman and built up his trust and his strength until they could find him a wonderful permanent home and Juliette used to meet up with her regularly with Norman and go for walks. In this time of course, Lilian fell madly in love with Norman and couldn't bear the thought of letting him go elsewhere, so her original thoughts of never wanting a dog had been quashed, once and for all.

We spent the most delightful hour listening to the stories and reminiscing. I went from roaring with laughter one minute, to wiping away a tear the next when emotion overwhelmed me. I learnt so much about Aunty Lil's physical presence, her huge heart, her 'never say never spirit', and how she would never let anything stand in her way. I know not every meeting would be like this, but what a way to kick-start to my WI initiation. I loved it.

Joan and Val stood once more at the front of

the hall and invited me to join them while they presented me with a framed embroidery with Aunt Lilian's name, the dates of her life and the WI logo. Underneath her name, it said the words:

Lilian Wagstaff
treasured member of Muddleford WI
now and always
never forgotten.

We all stood and sang 'Jerusalem'. I was glad I'd looked up the words the night before as I only knew the first line up till then. It felt a bit strange with everyone's eyes on me. When the song finished, Val asked me to chat about our beach-hut soiree.

'So, when I was told that Norman, the love of Aunty Lil's life' – a little ripple of laughter went around the room – 'came from a dog rescue centre, which may now have to close down due to a lack of funding, I wanted to see how I could help and how Aunty Lil could leave a legacy behind her. So I'd like to invite you all to join us at her beach hut on Muddleford Beach two weeks on Thursday for a fabulous swishing event.'

There were confused looks around the room. Clearly swishing hadn't reached the Dorset coast. That was good. At least it would be a unique event and if it turned out to be an absolute shambles no-one would know any different. I'd spoken to Rita on the phone a day ago and she'd very kindly given me some fabulous advice about how she ran events before she got her shop up and running.

'Swishing is where you bring along unwanted clothes and swap them for something else. Then if you don't have anything to swap, but there's something that you want, you make a donation for each additional item. We are looking for stock in advance too, so if you'd like to donate anything to the event, I'd love to hear from you. I didn't know what to do with Aunty Lil's clothes so there will be lots of items from her wardrobes. She had some amazing clothes and I'd love them to find new wonderful homes where they'll still be worn and maybe even treasured.'

'Oh how wonderful,' spoke up one lady in the audience who'd introduced herself earlier as Jill. 'Lilian was always so beautifully dressed and, as I said earlier, I admired her dress sense very much and always used to say to her that I'd love a good old rummage in her wardrobe.'

I smiled at the thought of Jill rooting through Aunty Lil's wardrobe.

'So we're looking for donations of clothes – which must be in excellent condition – jewellery, scarves, bags and shoes. You can either bring them along on the night, or drop them off beforehand. If you want to do that, please call me to arrange it. I'll sort out a time to meet you at the hut. We will be selling tickets for the event at £2.50 per ticket, you can buy a glass of bubbly for the same price, and we thought that we'd set the item price at £2.50 too to make it nice and easy. We'd love to see as many of you as possible there on the evening. I do hope you can join us. Please do tell all your friends about it and bring them along too to help to make it a fabulous event. '

Pamela yelled from the back row, 'Do you have a poster? I can put one up in the shop.'

'Ooh me too,' piped up Karen from the hair-dresser's. 'Or some leaflets that I can give out to my customers?'

'I'll get Walter to give out some in the butcher's shop to all the ladies that come in. And we can drop them in the delivery bags too.'

'Thank you so much, ladies. You've all been very generous.'

My heart swelled. These people didn't know me at all, but they were doing this for Aunty Lil and one of the many causes that she supported.

'We're very excited about the event, Nell. We do love to do something for our local community and it will be wonderful to keep the shelter running for as long as we can with any money that we make. Lilian would be so very proud of you.' Joan squeezed my hand.

A lump formed in my throat and I could only mumble thanks and return to my seat. Oh how I wish she were here with me; knowing me later in my life and us spending quality time together. I felt so sad and still held so much regret. I wasn't sure whether that feeling would ever go.

Val came and sat next to me and rubbed my back. 'Don't be sad, darling. That's the last thing she would have wanted you to be. You can't change the past, but you can change the future. She left you what she did so that you can make a difference in the same way she did. She made her peace with losing touch with you and your mother a very long time ago. It took her a while initially, but once she did, she was a different person. I won't say she wasn't devastated at first because she was. And she tried so hard to get in touch with your mother, but she was having none of it. She'd have loved to see you sitting here today amongst her friends. I for one am so glad to have you back in our little world, and Jack was delighted when I told him that you'd come home. He's been away this week, with Natalia, but they'll be back tomorrow and I know he'll be desperate to see you.'

Finding that hard to believe after he'd spent the week away with the stunning Natalia, I wondered how we would act around each other. We would have to find our own new normal. Find a way to be just friends. After all, that's what we used to be. I wondered if they'd been abroad. Would Natalia have been prancing around on a beach in a skimpy bikini with her arse hanging out. Why did people do that? Are they really that vain that they think their arse is so beautiful that others would want to look at it?

Would Natalia have told him about our conversation at lunch or would she have kept it to herself?. My face flushed at the thought of him believing that I still held a torch for him after all these years. I gulped. As if!

Chapter Twenty-Nine

SITTING ON THE bed in Aunty Lil's room to go through her costume jewellery made me feel very nostalgic. There were a few items that brought back memories of me being here all those years ago. We'd spend hours going through her jewellery chest and she'd tell me stories of where she'd bought them or who had passed them on to her or for what occasion she'd worn them. She was a fabulous storyteller who kept me mesmerised with her captivating tales for hours on end. Most people had petite little jewellery boxes and she did have one of those for her valuable pieces, 'her real diamonds' she used to call them, but she had so much costume jewellery, it was all kept really well organised in a big old blanket chest and going through it and listening to her stories used to be one of my favourite things to do when I stayed at the house.

I hoped she wouldn't mind me getting rid of her things. I picked up a long necklace with a cornflower-blue pendant on the end which was absolutely stunning. I slid it over my head. The colour was a very close match to the dress I was wearing. Dresses seemed to be my new uniform down here. Along with cardigans and flip-flops. Long gone were the business suits and high heels I used to wear every day. It was lovely to be comfy in my clothes, which in turn made me feel comfortable in my skin. As the saying goes, life did definitely feel better in flip-flops.

There were still lots of gorgeous vintage-type items that I wanted to hang onto and wear myself but those things that weren't suitable or didn't fit were being put into her old shopping bag on wheels, ready to take down to the beach hut for our Beach Hut Swishing Event. I'd already had a good few messages from people wanting to drop stuff off to me so had arranged to be there between 12 and 4. I just hoped that we'd have enough stuff for the event.

Hammering on the front door disturbed me from my thoughts and I went to open it.

'Hey, gorgeous, it's so good to have you back.' Jack walked into the hallway, leaned in for a hug, then instead picked me up and twirled me around. 'I can't tell you how happy I am that you decided to come back.' He nuzzled into my neck.

This action really confused me. How could someone who felt the way his girlfriend said he did – that I was a pain – behave in this way? He really did seem truly delighted to see me, which is exactly what Val had said too. I breathed him in. He'd clearly come fresh from the shower as the back of his hair was wet and he smelt of sandalwood and citrus mixed with a tinge of cinnamon. He hugged me so tightly and didn't seem to want to let go. I melted into his arms, they had always made me feel safe and secure. But once more those words that Natalia had said to me flooded my thoughts and I gently extricated myself from him and moved away. I could do this.

'Ooh is that your gorgeous coffee on the go that I can smell, Nellie-bum? I could murder a mug! It's been a long old week.'

The smell which permanently filled the house, was a dead giveaway and I couldn't really deny it. I had to get a grip and just get on with being friends with him.

He stepped forward again and fingered the necklace I was wearing, accidentally and very lightly brushing his hand gently against my breast. My whole body tingled even though I knew it was unintentional.

'Pretty! It matches your beautiful eyes perfectly.' Showing no sign of embarrassment, as quickly as he picked it up, he dropped it again and walked through into the kitchen. God it was no wonder I was so confused when just the touch of his hand made me feel that way. Imagine if we… No, Nellie. Don't even go there.

A little more flushed than I intended, I went into the kitchen to see Jack on the floor with Norman giving him a belly rub. Norman was in ecstasy. But to be honest, I probably would have been too! Stop it, Nell!

'So did you have a good time on your holiday?' I asked as I turned my back on him and poured us both a coffee.

'Oh, it wasn't a holiday, it was a conference. About how we can make the practice better. That's why Natalia came too. I think she thought she was going to have a week of partying and staying up late, but I went to every lecture I could and lapped up what other people are doing to make their practice the best it can be. If she did party and stay up late, she certainly didn't do it with me.' He laughed.

Now I was even more confused. If they were staying together in a hotel room, how would he not know what she was doing. Or was he just not telling me the truth. I really couldn't work it out.

'So tell me, what made you come back? Was it the fact that now you've found me again, you couldn't bear to be apart?' He laughed nervously.

'Oh, it's a long story. And really not important. But I have made the decision to move down for the time being and just run with it.'

'Honestly, Nellie-bum, I'm so happy you made this decision. When Mum told me, I was so excited. Think about all the fun we can have together. All the stuff we can do. And hey, who knows what the future holds.' He looked at me and stared deep into my eyes. I couldn't tear mine away from his. It felt as if he could see deep into the very soul of me. There were so many unspoken words between us.

Norman came up and nudged Jack's hand and the moment was broken when he laughed and looked down at him and stroked his head. I had never felt so conflicted. How could he behave this way with me, when he was clearly in a relationship with Natalia and she had told me what he'd said? I really needed to talk this out with Shivani again.

'Mum's told me all about your project to help the shelter. I'm so grateful to you for doing this, Nellie-bum. It's so kind of you to want to raise funds. I know Lilian would have been delighted with what you are doing. She was such a huge supporter once she'd met Norman there and had been helping out both financially and physically as much as she could at her age. I hated asking for her help, but she'd insist on coming down to the shelter even if it was just to sit with some of the dogs and brush them and give them her time.'

'How did she get involved with it, Jack?'

'Why don't we go for a walk on the beach after our coffees and I can tell you all about it. And you can tell me all about your event and I'll have a think about how we can help at the vet's too.'

Norman's ears pricked up at the word 'walk' and he started dancing around Jack's feet. He was such a funny little thing. Walking would be good. Walking side by side was much easier than sitting opposite him, as I didn't have to look into those gorgeous eyes and get lost in a world that would never be mine.

We walked and talked. Jack told me how Aunty Lil had started helping out at the shelter when they'd taken in a dog that needed some care and Jack was struggling to get them looked after. How after then, she'd met Norman, who at six months old had been too much for the family that had him when the lady fell pregnant and with two young children already, couldn't cope with a dog too. Lilian fell utterly and madly in love with

Norman and it had given her a new lease of life.

I loved hearing stories about Aunty Lil. It made her come alive again in my head. For me that meant the Aunty Lil who was only sixty years old and was full of life, although it sounded like even in her eighties, she still was. If I could always remember her like that, I'd be happy. I'm glad in a way that I didn't get to see her age, have aches and pains and get old. She would always be eternally youthful in my mind.

We talked about the swishing event and Jack had some good ideas too.

'You know you should tell Natalia of your plans. While she's a good practice manager, the one thing that she knows even more about is fashion, and her sister is a colour consultant and personal shopper and she might like to be involved in the event in some way. It might generate some business for her too. What do you think?'

'I'm not sure, Jack. I don't think Natalia is particularly fond of me, to be honest.'

'Really? She's only ever been nice about you to me. I was going to ask you about going back up to the Midlands though. She did say that you had some unfinished business with a man you had to deal with. I hope you got everything sorted out.'

God, she couldn't wait to tell him that. Put him

off the scent I suppose. She obviously adored Jack and couldn't bear the thought of someone taking him away. I suppose if you loved someone that much then you'd do anything to keep them. I did think I needed to reassure her that I would be happy just to be Jack's friend. And hopefully hers too.

I'd drifted off a little while Jack was still talking but caught the bit where he said he would make sure to ask Natalia to include the swishing event in a newsletter to all their clients as quickly as possible and that he'd also put up posters on the noticeboards in the practice. He very kindly offered us the use of the practice printer. I'd always been involved in creating artwork in my previous job, so I was confident I could knock up an eye-catching poster. He also said that he would mention the event to all the staff too, in the hope that they'd come along, bring friends and donate items.

If everyone who we'd asked actually turned up, it would be amazing, though I knew that probably wouldn't be the case. But we could only worry about the things that we could control, which was making sure that everyone who did turn up had a fabulous time and that there was plenty of stock to go round. All we had to do was pray for good weather and a good turnout.

Chapter Thirty

WITH JUST A week to go, the beach hut was absolutely rammed with stock. There was certainly no need for me to worry about what we'd have to sell, and lots of people were getting in touch to ask whether it would be OK if they brought things along on the day. There were piles and piles of clothes, handbags and boxes of shoes. The WI had a couple of gazebos we'd use on the day and the forecast for the next week or so was unbroken sunshine, so we just hoped that the forecasters had got it right for once.

Dom's legal practice had very kindly donated twenty bottles of Buck's Fizz and so far ticket sales had reached over fifty, which I was very pleased with. The local bakery was making some cakes to sell on the evening and it all looked like it was heading for a success. I was delighted. And knackered! But also overwhelmed with joy and satisfaction. This was my idea coming to fruition.

I looked at my watch. It was time to head off. I

popped Norman back to the house, much to his disgust, although I knew he'd be napping before I'd even driven the car off the drive.

When I pulled up at the cafe, I cringed, remembering the last time I was there. This time I'd made sure I arrived first. I needed to have the upper hand in any way I possibly could.

Seated right by the window, so I could see when she arrived, I looked out over the quay. Families were crabbing, children with buckets and spades in one hand, ice creams in the other, following parents laden down with beach bags and picnic blankets heading to the beach. The boat that took people over to the little island opposite the quay for daytrips was running. I loved everything about being here. I just had to get over this little hurdle.

The bell over the door dinged, and I could smell her perfume and knew she'd arrived. I stood to greet her and held out my hand before she could air kiss me. I wanted to be resolute and get the situation cleared up without any falseness of being besties, which we clearly weren't.

'Hi, Natalia. It's lovely to see you. Do sit. Can I get you some water while we're waiting?'

She seemed a little on the back foot. Good, that's exactly how I wanted her to feel.

'I'd like to say something before lunch. To clear the air between us and clear up any misunderstandings.'

She nodded, even though I purposefully hadn't asked a question. I'm not sure where this assertive Nellie had come from but I liked her.

'I feel like we haven't got off to a good start, Natalia—'

She went to speak but I held up my palm to stop her. She bit her lip.

'I'm not sure what impression I gave before I went away, but I want you to know that I have no designs on Jack at all, and that all I want is for him to be happy. I'm not the type of girl to take another woman's man. I'm a woman's woman. I'd like to think that I'm a good friend and I'm loyal.'

She looked at me with her steely eyes, giving nothing away. Not even a hint of what she was thinking.

'I'd like you and I to be friends, not enemies. I think we'd be good for each other. I am actually quite nice if you gave me a chance. And I think you are amazing. You're clearly fantastic at your job, you are beautiful...' I could see her physically preening at this point. 'I'd absolutely love your help when it comes to the swishing event. You know fashion, you always look amazing and I know you love animals too. I'd love to join forces with you, Natalia, and ask you for your help in raising as much money as we can from this event for the dog shelter. I think you are the perfect person to help. And if you don't want to do it for me, then please think about the dogs.' I felt like I had nothing else to offer or say. I hoped I'd remembered everything I'd rehearsed before I got here. 'What do you say?'

She intertwined her hands and rested her chin on them and gazed at me.

'So you don't fancy Jack, then?'

'I do not fancy Jack.' I bit my lip. 'He's really not my type.'

'And you're not in love with him?'

I gulped. 'I am absolutely *not* in love with him.' I crossed my fingers underneath the table. Perhaps if I said it enough times, I'd start to believe it myself.

'And you think I'm beautiful?'

'I really do. You said yourself, why would Jack ever look at me when he has you? Why have a burger, when you can have steak?' Seriously. Who was I trying to kid? I may have overdone it a little there.

'OK, I'll help! Let's have a drink to seal the deal.' She tittered. 'I have some great ideas, Nellie. I've been thinking about them since Jack mentioned the event and I really think they would help to raise even more money.'

'Great, let's have them. But first, I'm starving. Let's order some food.' This time when I ordered a pasta dish, I didn't feel at all guilty. I didn't feel like I was on show for someone to approve of me like I had the last time. I felt like I was being me. Just me. I'd grown enough over the last few weeks to be just me.

We talked through loads of ideas over lunch. It was really enjoyable and she was actually very good company. She was really animated when talking about her sister, who she clearly adored, and how she could get her involved with make-up demos and making it into a proper girl's night out. I loved her ideas and we made lots of plans. We wrote lots of lists and we had many jobs to go away and make happen. I was so glad that I had asked her for help. I hoped that, finally, she didn't feel threatened by me. We really could be a good team and make things happen.

She smiled at me across the table. When she smiled she was actually very pretty. She just needed to lose the caked-on make-up. She really didn't need it. If she just let herself relax a bit more and loosen up, and not be so defensive, then I really did hope we could be friends. I was genuinely excited about what the future held.

Chapter Thirty-One

NATALIA HAD TURNED a tide. She'd been an absolute rock to me in the days following our lunch. Her and her sister, Miranda, had been to the beach hut many times since to help out and to bring loads of clothes that people had dropped off at the vet's. Miranda had some clothes rails which would come in fantastically helpful, along with some shelving units for display purposes. And four female mannequins, about which I wasn't even going to ask where she'd got them or why.

The event was just one night away so we didn't have long to get everything prepared. The biggest problem I had was that I felt we might have too much stock and not enough people to come along. I had no idea what I'd do if I was stuck with loads of clothes. Good job Aunty Lil's house had many spare rooms. Although Joan had just called to say that there'd been seventy-five tickets sold, which I was really pleased about.

'Good evening, would you be Miss Ellen Wagstaff?'

I jumped at the unexpected sound of a deep voice behind me. Stood in front of me was a policeman. A very tall, handsome one. What on earth could he want with me?

'It has come to our attention, Miss Wagstaff, that you are running a business from this beach hut.'

'Erm no. Actually I'm not. We are having a charity event tomorrow evening. It's definitely not a business.'

'Well, it's been reported to us that you are running a business.'

'Absolutely not. Here's a leaflet to say what's happening. Perhaps you have a girlfriend, or a wife or mother who might like to come along. It's a fab ladies' event. And we're raising money for the local dog shelter. Someone reported it? Can I ask who?'

'I'm not at liberty to disclose that information, I'm afraid. I've been told that food and drink will be on sale. I'm afraid that's not allowed from these beach huts because the beach is very much a public place.'

At that moment, Natalia came tottering along the promenade in her four-inch heels. 'Coooeee! I'm here Nellie.'

I watched the officer closely. His eyes nearly popped out of his head when he scanned Natalia's body, from her long tanned legs, micro skirt, white blouse and perfectly made-up face with poker-straight black hair. He loosened his tie a little.

'And you are?' he asked.

'Ooh hello, officer!' She winked at me. 'Natalia Fox at your service.' She held her hand out to him. Then she grabbed his arm. 'Oh my! Look at those muscles. You're so strong.'

He blushed but smiled.

'Is everything OK?' Natalia asked.

'There has been a report of the illegal use of a beach hut.'

'Oh how ridiculous.'

'It might seem ridiculous but you absolutely cannot sell alcohol from these premises without a liquor licence.'

I put my hand to my mouth. I'd never even given that a thought.

'How about if we were to give it away instead? Would that be allowed?' Natalia asked.

'Well, as long as the drinks were consumed mainly on the premises, and no money changes hands, and there's no drunken debauchery taking place...' He raised his eyebrow at Natalia and she winked at him and licked her lips. 'Then I'm sure that can be overlooked.'

Natalia took his arm and turned him away

towards the café. 'Can I buy you a coffee, Officer...?'

'Sergeant James.'

'Well, Sergeant James,' she purred. 'Let's go and discuss all of this over a coffee.' She winked at me over her shoulder. 'Be back later, Nellie.'

I laughed as she walked off up the beach. Jack really was going to have his work cut out with her as a wife. She was a born flirt. Though I hoped she'd get everything sorted out that we needed. We couldn't afford to have any issues this late in the day.

I was packing the final stuff away, when she returned looking a little flustered.

'Well...?' I asked.

'Oh gosh, what a hottie he is. I've discovered he doesn't have a girlfriend or a wife but he is going to ask his mother and two sisters to come along tomorrow night.'

I laughed. 'Oh, Natalia, I'm sure you could sell sand to Arabs.'

She tittered. 'Oh well, it looks like everything is sorted. The only issue we could have is that while you were planning to charge for drinks tomorrow night, you are now going to have to give them away. But it's not the end of the world. We'll just have to try harder to sell more stuff to make up for it.'

'Thanks so much for offering to do that.'

'It was my absolute pleasure.' She smirked back at me.

Sleep evaded me that night. I had a bad feeling in the pit of my stomach and kept waking. I stood at the window, looking out across the sea, watching the moon's reflection on it, making sparkles. So pretty.

When I eventually did catch a few hours and woke a little later, Norman and I went down to the beach bright and early to start our day. I hoped the fresh air would energise me for a busy day and night ahead.

Our normal game of catch and fetch on the beach was fun. There were not many people about and after half an hour I called Norman over, not sure who was panting more, and headed off to the beach hut. As we approached, I could see a small gathering of people at the doors and, lo and behold, Sergeant James standing with his record book in his hand, writing notes. I ran towards the hut, Norman trailing behind me.

The locks had been cropped off and what I saw of the inside, made me fall to my knees. All of Aunty Lil's stuff had been upended and tipped all over the floor, and it looked like there were quite a few boxes missing. On the doors to the hut, someone had painted the words: *'Take your flips and flop off! You're not welcome round here'* in bright-red paint.

All our hard work down the pan. All the proceeds which were going to charity, would now not happen. All the effort that everyone had gone to, to make this a success. Gone.

Tears streamed down my cheeks as I looked at the damage that had been done.

And that was the moment that I blacked out.

The smell of ammonia, shoved up my nose, brought me round pretty damn quickly. I looked up to find Val above me and Jack at my side.

'What the…?'

'Mum's tried and tested remedy,' said Jack. 'Smelling salts. Sorry about that. How are you feeling now? You must have had a bit of a shock, Nellie-bum.'

Norman was leaning into my side and I gave him a pat.

'I'm just so upset. We won't be able to have the event tonight. The whole thing has been spoilt.'

'I do hope you are not going to give up that easily.'

KIM NASH

'What else can we do?'

'Well, while you've been having a little nap, we've been busy arranging a little something ourselves.'

'What? Tell me?'

'I think you'd just better wait and see. I think you'll be surprised at the community spirit around here.'

Val tried to prop me up, and Jack gave me his hand.

'Come on, lazy bum. Get your bearings back then you and Mum are going off to the café for a cup of hot sweet tea, and you'll soon be feeling much better.'

'I need to have a look and see what's missing.'

Natalia appeared from the back of the beach hut. I hadn't realised she was here. She must have come down with Jack.

'I'm sorry, Nellie, but an awful lot of Lilian's stuff has been taken,' she said.

I put my head in my hands. 'No!' I felt a bubble of emotion well up inside me. 'No, not Aunty Lil's stuff. Please.'

'I'm sorry, Nellie,' said Jack.

I crumpled against him and he held me up. I looked across at Natalia and she was watching us very closely. She wandered over to where Sergeant

James was stood and started talking to him in a low voice. He scribbled something down, closed his notebook, raised his hand towards me and walked away along the promenade.

Feeling a little brighter now I'd taken in the news and had got back on my feet, I agreed to walk to the café with Val. We sat for over an hour, drinking endless sweet tea, me going over and over again why anyone could do such a thing and why someone had it in for me. The only person who hadn't been friendly towards me had been Natalia and even she was on my side these days.

While I was sat there with Val, I thought it would be a good opportunity to raise the issue of the falling out between Mum and Aunty Lilian. But then I changed my mind. It seemed like we had enough on our plate right now without bringing that up. However, Val must have sensed there was still something on my mind, and she asked if it was anything she could help with. Here was my opportunity.

'Do you know why Mum and Aunty Lil fell out, Val? It's really playing on my mind. I feel like I'm never going to know and I'm driving myself mad looking for a clue and not finding anything.'

Val frowned. 'I think you and I should have a proper chat about this but I don't think that right now is the best time. I think we need longer with no interruptions. How about we meet up and have a cuppa in the next few days and I'll tell you everything I know.'

'Thank you.' I reached across and hugged her. My heart felt a little lighter. I felt I was finally going to find out the mystery behind why my life had changed so much.

But right then, we had an event to get prepared for.

When we arrived back at the beach hut, what I saw brought a smile to my face and a tear to my eye. Dom and Tom were laughing as they frantically painted over the red words, in the exact same pastel shade of blue that the beach hut had previously been, but because it was new paint it was brighter and more vivid. You couldn't see the words any longer. The bunting that had been pulled down had been put back in its place and fairy lights plugged in around it. Joan and Natalia were busy sorting all the clothes that had been pulled onto the floor and Miranda was steaming the creases out of them and hanging them straight onto the rails. It was 11 a.m. and the event was starting at 5 p.m. We had six hours to see if we could locate some more stock. Natalia had put a call into the vet's and the staff there were doing all they could along with the WI members that Joan had roped in too. But what finally tipped me over the edge was when Sergeant James appeared with three disgruntled-looking teenagers who were carrying two boxes each of Aunty Lil's clothes. He winked at Natalia and she came over to me.

'I owe you a huge apology, Nellie. *Huge.*' She grabbed the largest of the boys by the ear and dragged him over to me. 'This is my stupid little brother. He overheard something he shouldn't have, and assumed something he shouldn't have. And he has something to say to you.'

'I'm really very sorry that we did this. I'm an idiot and I'll be paying for it for the rest of my life.' He looked at his sister and glared. 'Let go of my fecking ear!'

She let him go and the three of them sloped off. I was really very puzzled by what he'd said but the important thing was that all the clothes had been returned and by the look of it all intact too.

'I have some explaining to do to you later, Nellie, but for now, let's get cracking on getting everything ready and have the brilliant evening that this was always going to be. I'll explain all tomorrow, I promise.'

It was getting more baffling by the minute but I didn't have the time or the energy to think about it now. We had an event to get ready for!

Chapter Thirty-Two

TWO HOURS TO go and there was lots to do. Even Sergeant James had returned in his civilian clothes, in which he looked mighty fine I might add, and was putting up the gazebos and carrying the weights over to anchor them down. We'd borrowed as many chairs as we could from the church hall and Jack had transported them in his pickup truck, but they still needed bringing down to the beach. Natalia had enlisted the help of her little brother and his errant friends, which she said was the least they could do.

Miranda had dressed the mannequins in beautiful boho outfits which you would never have thought second-hand for one minute. They stood to one side of the doors while a makeshift bar that Dom and Tom had somehow put together out of old pallets that they'd painted in beach-hut blue, with glasses waiting on trays to be filled.

As I stood taking some photos of the set-up, although I knew I'd never forget this sight for as long as I lived, a voice that I would know anywhere spoke up.

'What does a girl have to do to get a drink round here?'

'Oh! My! God! What the hell are you doing here?' I screamed and flung myself on Shivani. 'Why didn't you tell me you were coming?'

'Well, then that wouldn't be a surprise now would it. And I know you don't like surprises. Remember the time when—'

'Could someone please get this wonderful lady a drink. *Now!*' I squeezed her again for good measure. 'Oh, Shivani, I can't tell you how happy I am to see you.'

'Well, I couldn't let an event like this go ahead without being here for you could I? I was hoping to be here earlier, but I struggled to get away. I've literally just come from the station. Can I put my bag somewhere? Can I do anything to help?'

'I think it's all in hand, to be honest. With an hour to go I think everything is finally done.'

'Well, that's what you call perfect timing.'

At that point Jack wandered over. He and Natalia had been quite distanced from each other today and I wondered whether something had been said.

'Jack, this is my very best friend in the whole

world, Shivani.'

'Oh, that's quite hurtful. There was me thinking that I was your very best friend in the whole
world, Nellie-bum. But anyway, it's lovely to meet
you Shivani. I was just coming over to say why
don't you go back to the house and get yourself
ready, Nellie. I know you said you wanted to get
quickly showered and changed before kick-off.' He
glanced at his watch. 'You've got about an hour at
my reckoning.'

'It's nice to meet you too, Jack. You are exactly
as I imagined you to be.'

I felt the heat burning up inside of me. Please
do not embarrass me, I pleaded to her with my
eyes.

'Yes, you are everything she said you were.'

I grabbed her by her arm and swung her round.

'Thanks so much, Jack, we'll be back in a bit.'

'Fuck me, Nell, you never told me he was a
God!' she said as we walked away.

'Ssshhh, you nutter. He'll hear you.'

I turned and looked behind me and Jack was
watching us walk away. He raised his hand in a
little wave. My heart skipped.

'And I think you'd better tell me why the fuck
he calls you "Nellie-bum" too!'

'WOW-FUCKING-WEE! THIS HOUSE is huge. And totally gorgeous. Why on earth did you reconsider coming back to the Midlands when you get to look at that view every day?' Shivani asked as she looked out the lounge window.

I was beginning to wonder that myself. I felt more at home there each day.

'I'll give you the full tour when we get back later but right now, I need to jump in the shower and get ready. Help yourself to anything you want. There's another bathroom on the ground floor and I'll be as quick as I can. Can you just do me a favour and let Norman out for a wee, please?'

'Will do, babe. I'm just going to sit and look at the view.'

Hanging on the back of my bedroom door was a dress I'd discovered right at the back of Aunty Lil's wardrobe. I knew as soon as I saw it that I wanted to wear it for the event. The fitted bodice was made from taffeta and then the pleated chiffon skirt skimmed over my hips and draped to just below the knee. I slipped on some little kitten heels with diamantes on the front in a practically identical colour. I was so glad at that moment that I was the same size as Aunty Lil in both clothes and shoes. She had fabulous style and wearing this dress made me feel a million dollars. As I swirled down the staircase, Shivani wolf-whistled at me and I did a twirl.

'Babe, you look hot as hell tonight! He'll never keep his eyes off you.'

'Who?'

'Who do you think? I haven't been your friend for twenty years to not know that you are head over heels in love with Jack. And he looks at you the same way.'

'Don't be silly, Shivani. He's with Natalia.'

'Don't tell me she's the one with all the fake tan who I saw on a bench at the top of the beach steps, with her tongue down the back of some beefy guy's throat.'

'Oh my god. That must be Sergeant James. She must be cheating on Jack with him.' I looked at my watch. 4.50 p.m. We had to go. The event was about to start. I hadn't time to worry about that. 'Come on, let's go! Oh no! Where's Norman?'

'He was sitting on the chair in the lounge when I looked a few seconds ago. Come on, you can't be late to your own event.'

'Bye, Norman, won't be long darling,' I yelled as we slammed the front door behind us.

As we ran down the steps to the beach, all you could hear was the hum of chatter and all you could see was a queue of people lining up to get to the beach hut. There must have been at least a hundred people. Natalia hauled me over. 'Come on, quick. You need to declare the event open. You need to say a few words.'

I was totally unprepared for what lay before me. Fairy lights lined the beach hut and the two large gazebos around them. There were table displays of jewellery, bags and shoes and rails and rails of clothes. Tables and chairs were dotted around with bottles with fairy lights inside them made wonderful centrepieces. It all looked so pretty. Natalie thrust a glass of Buck's Fizz into one of my hands and a microphone in the other. Jack helped me up onto a milk crate so I could see everyone and they could see me.

'Erm, I just wanted to say thank you, for making this event possible. We're here this evening to raise money for the Fantastic Furries Dog Shelter, which is a cause that was very close to Aunty Lil's heart.' A lump appeared in my throat and I had to swallow it down before I could continue. 'I'd love to raise as much as we can in honour of Aunty Lil. Please do grab a glass of complimentary Buck's Fizz and browse the goods. If you've already donated items, you will have a number on your ticket which will tell you how many items you can take. Anything above that number, will be charged at £2.50 an item. I'd like to thank you all for coming along to this swishing event. And I suppose it just leaves me to say, enjoy your evening and let's get swishing.'

A round of applause followed and the crowd surged forward. Jack helped me down from the crate.

People were picking clothes up off the rails already and I could see things exchanging hands with lots of oohs and aahs. There were so many clothes hanging up, all sorted into sizes and some even with tags still on that had never been worn.

Jack was still holding my hands and turned to face me. 'Nellie-bum. You are stunning tonight. And I'm so super proud of everything that you have achieved here. Look what you have done.'

I looked around me, but couldn't get the words that he'd said out of my head. He'd told me I looked stunning. How on earth was I supposed to react to that? He couldn't keep confusing me this way. I couldn't stand it any longer. I was going to have to say something for my own sanity.

'Jack, you have no right to say these things to me.'

'What?' He frowned. 'Why not? They're all true.'

'Because of you and Natalia. You can't be with

her and say these things to me. You can't look at me the way you do. You can't play with my feelings like this and it's not fair on her either.'

I turned to walk away but he grabbed my hand and looked deep into my eyes.

'I don't know what you think is going on with me and Natalia, but I can assure you that it's nothing. She told me earlier about the time she took you out for lunch and warned you away from me. I had no idea she felt that way towards me and I had no idea she had said those things to you, until she told me this afternoon. I'm sorry that she said what she did, but surely you know me by now, Nellie-bum,' he said in a low voice, his eyes never moving from mine.

He tucked a stray hair behind my ear, and his hand brushed against my face. I closed my eyes and breathed him in.

'I loved you all those years ago, Nellie-bum, and I couldn't bring myself to tell you then. I don't think I ever stopped. I promised myself that I'd let you get away once and that you wouldn't ever get away from me again.'

I heard music start to play. When I turned around, Tom had set himself up with a guitar and an amplifier. He had the voice of an angel and the song he was singing was another of Aunty Lil's favourites – 'The Way You Look Tonight'.

The sun was starting to set, the sky was turning dark blue. Friends surrounded me laughing and drinking, and had helped my little dream come to fruition. Everything was picture-perfect.

'Dance with me.'

Jack held out his hand and I looked deep into his eyes. I knew that everything he was saying was the truth. I took his hand and moved in close.

He whispered into my ear, 'I love you, Nellie-bum. I always have and I always will.'

When his lips met mine, a million fireworks erupted in my tummy. The kiss was everything I thought it would be and more. Just twenty years later than originally planned. But spectacularly worth the wait.

Chapter Thirty-Three

TIDYING UP HAD taken a while but with so many of us helping, it was much quicker than I thought. The evening had been a huge success and we'd raised well over two hundred and fifty pounds on ticket prices alone. The price from the swishing came to just over twelve hundred and fifty pounds. We had lots of delighted customers who had gone away with bags and bags of new clothes. And we'd also had some generous donations from local businesses who'd wanted to help. We needed to do a proper count up of everything tomorrow but I reckoned we'd raised at least fifteen hundred pounds which was pretty good going for our first event.

Shivani had been an absolute trooper on the clearing-up front, working hard to get everything donc. Natalia asked if she could see me tomorrow as she had a lot of things to explain, so we arranged to meet for lunch before she wandered off hand in hand with Sergeant James whose first name turned out to be Reginald. No wonder he stuck to Sergeant James as much as he could.

Jack flung his arm around my shoulder as we sauntered back to Aunty Lil's house. It had been an exhausting day but I don't think I'd ever felt so proud of anything I'd achieved and I don't think I'd ever felt happier.

Norman was normally waiting by the front door as soon as he heard the key in the lock but unusually there was no sign of him. I wandered into the lounge and summer room calling him, but couldn't find him anywhere. Shivani said she'd look in the kitchen while I scoured the bedrooms, in case he'd got himself shut into any of the rooms, but he was nowhere to be found. My heart began thumping harder and harder as I called his name but there was no pitter patter of his feet to be heard anywhere.

'Norman? Norman?' My voice was becoming more fretful by the second. Where the hell was he?

'Nell, I think you'd better come down to the kitchen.'

My heart sank. Sometimes you can just tell by the tone of someone's voice that something is wrong and I knew it at that moment – Jack's voice was flatter than I'd ever heard it before. I flew down the stairs, nearly missing the last few in my haste.

As I raced into the kitchen, the back door was wide open. Shivani was sat at the kitchen table with tears running down her cheeks and looking horrified.

'I'm so sorry, Nell. You asked me to put him out for a wee and I assumed he'd come back in. But I've just been out in the garden and the back gate was open. I did see the window cleaner here earlier and meant to mention it but with all the rush of getting out on time, I just forgot all about it. They must have left the gate open. I'm so sorry, Nell, but I think he must have got out.'

Jack went to comfort me, but I shoved him aside and fled out into the garden calling Norman's name at the top of my voice. There wasn't a soul in sight as I ran out of the gate, frantically searching up and down. Blood was pumping through my veins so quickly as I ran towards the shops, scouring the gardens and hedges all the while. But there was no sign of him anywhere.

Shivani ran in the opposite direction. I knew how awful she must be feeling right now but I couldn't even think about her feelings. I just wanted to find Norman. Wherever he was he might be frightened and thinking he was going to be told off. I tried not to screech his name, but instead call him cheerfully, as if he was just in the garden, so he wouldn't be scared to come back.

'Come on Norman, where are you boy? Are you coming for a biscuit?' The word biscuit was normally a sure thing to get him running straight to me from anywhere. But there was nothing.

As I got nearer to the house again, I spotted the woods at the bottom of the road and got an awful feeling. Surely he wouldn't have gone in there. He didn't normally go in that direction, but I had a feeling deep inside my tummy and it wasn't a good one. I picked up my pace and started searching around the bushes, repeatedly calling his name, trying to keep the panic from my voice.

Suddenly, I heard a whimpering sound. I stopped to make sure there was no other noise, to see if I could hear it again. There it was, a faint whine.

'Norman? Norman?'

There it was again, a strained noise. The awful noise of someone or something in pain. I ran towards the noise and searched frantically through the undergrowth and yelled for Jack, who quickly appeared behind me. There, under a tree, was my gorgeous Norman, who was covered with blood. His eyes were closed and I couldn't tell if he was alive. I gasped and looked at Jack, as he knelt on the ground and blew air through Norman's lips.

He then let out a huge sigh of relief as he put his hand over Norman's heart.

'He is breathing, but it doesn't look good, Nellie. Move over and let me take a look. In fact, can you go and get a blanket? Here're my keys too. Bring the pickup truck over. I think we need to get this fella to the surgery and see how much damage has been done. It looks like he's been hit by a car.'

'Oh my god. Norman, my darling. We'll get you sorted, sweetie. Oh you poor thing.' I went to stroke his head.

'Nellie, go now. We don't have any time to waste.'

'Oh Norman.'

'NOW, NELL! GO!'

When I came back with the truck, Jack jumped in the back seat with Norman.

'You'll have to drive,' he said.

'I can't drive this huge thing.'

'You don't have a choice, Nellie. I need to keep applying pressure to the wound. I'll sit on the back seat with him. Just get us there as quickly as you can.'

I took a deep breath and rammed the vehicle into drive. It was blooming huge and I'd only recently got used to driving again, let alone a bloody great truck. Thank god it was an automatic. I was trying to balance driving quickly with driving safely and not taking corners too quickly so that I didn't hurt Norman any more than he already was. It was all quite difficult when I was already shaking like a leaf.

Jack phoned ahead to the surgery and told the emergency team what had happened and to prep one of the operating theatres. It felt unusual to hear him in work mode. He was calm and authoritative and it felt good to know that he was in control.

'Pull up right outside the front doors, Nellie.'

I did as he asked and he jumped out the minute the truck came to a stop.

I turned to face him. 'Is he going to be OK, Jack?' I was almost scared to ask the question that was on the tip of my tongue. Norman didn't appear to be moving at all.

Jack looked me straight in the eye. 'It's not looking good, Nell. I'm so sorry. I can't make any promises but all I can say, Nellie, is that I'm going to do everything in my power to save him.'

I didn't realise that I was holding my breath as he lifted Norman from the back seat and carried him through to one of the rooms to the right of the yard. My whole body began to shake and Natalia appeared from nowhere and wrapped a shawl around my shoulders as she guided me towards the waiting room where she had a hot cup of sugary tea waiting for me. Shivani followed behind. I couldn't bring myself to even look at her, let alone speak to her. This was all her fault.

After ten minutes of sitting around counting the seconds ticking away on the clock, I had to get outside for some air. My chest felt tight and I couldn't get my breath. I'd left the house without my handbag so didn't even have my inhaler at hand. I crouched down to the floor and put my head between my knees barely balancing and remembering what my social worker had told me years ago, when I used to get panic attacks. I took a deep breath in through my nose until I couldn't fill my body any more with good air, and then breathed out through my mouth, pushing out all of the bad. After five breaths like this, my breathing regulated and within a few minutes returned to a normal pace. I felt calmer and more able to cope.

The sky was clear, and as I looked up at the stars there was one star, brighter than all of the others surrounding it. I didn't realise I could love a dog the way I did, but Norman had become my new everything.

'Please, Aunty Lil. I know you probably want him back with you, but we were just starting to make a really good life for ourselves. Please don't take him, not yet.'

Natalia was suddenly by my side. I'm not sure where she had come from again, she was in stealth mode I think.

'Jack has done all he can for the time being.' She held my hands within hers. 'All we can do now is wait.'

Chapter Thirty-Four

IT FELT LIKE hours had passed and I don't know how I could possibly have slept but when I woke, I was lying on a bench, Natalia was stroking my hair, and my head was bizarrely on her lap. Funny who has your back when you really need it. She'd been really very kind over the last few days. Reg was clearly good for her.

Natalia told me that she'd told Shivani to go home and get some sleep and that we'd call her as soon as we knew anything.

A door creaked open down the corridor and we all awaited the approaching soft footsteps which got louder and louder until Jack stood before us.

His face broke out into a smile. 'He's going to be OK, Nellie-bum. He's going to be OK.' He held his arms out to me.

'Thank you! Thank you! Thank you!' I jumped into his arms and wrapped my legs around him and as we fell backwards, I remembered that I was no waif as we hit the decks. Jack bumped his head on the bench behind him but, as a true gentleman, had broken my fall as I landed right on top of him with my face mere millimetres away from his. 'Jeez! I'm so sorry! Are you OK? Oh my god, Jack, what have I done? Jack! *Jack!*'

But no movement came from him at all. The poor guy might have just saved my dog, but in my excitement, I may have bloody killed him.

He shook his head and came to. 'For fuck's sake, Nellie-bum. What have you been eating lately?'

We both laughed out loud and I hoped that him cracking a joke meant that he'd forgiven me. He looked down at my lips and back to my eyes again questioningly. I leaned forward a tad and our lips met.

'Oh get a room you two!' Natalia laughed at the sorry state we'd ended up in and gave us both a hand up before wandering behind the reception desk. She seemed to find the whole situation hilarious.

'Can I see him?' I asked Jack.

'Walk this way, Miss Wagstaff.'

I giggled as he did a River-Dance style movement, and fake limped down the corridor. I loved how he sometimes reverted to that fourteen-year-old boy I adored. He always did know how to make me smile. Even at a time when my heart was in tatters.

Norman lifted his head from the bed he was lying on, and made a half-hearted attempt to wag his tail but after one thump, it all seemed like too much effort and he laid his head back down again.

'Can I?' I asked Jack, indicating the floor.

'Fill your boots!'

I crouched down on the floor next to Norman and gently stroked his head. He opened one big brown eye and then another and sniffed at my face, then gave me a big wet soggy lick. I know you shouldn't let dogs lick your face, especially after where they sniff and lick, but at that moment I couldn't have cared less.

'He lost so much blood, Nellie-bum, I really didn't think he was going to make it. We had to give him a blood transfusion and his injuries were quite severe. But by some small miracle, he fought and held on. He's going to need to stay in at least another night or two so the night nurses can keep an eye on him, but I reckon if he's still doing well after that, you can take him home.'

'I can't tell you how grateful I am, Jack.'

He wrapped his arms around me and kissed me again. Our lips moulded perfectly together. All my worries melted away.

'How grateful exactly? Care to show me just how much?'

I looked into those eyes that twinkled back at me. God, he was sexy even at 4 a.m. after a really traumatic time.

'Erm, extremely grateful.'

'Well obviously...' He dropped little butterfly kisses on my bottom lip, and a million fireworks exploded in my body. 'You may need some extra home-based veterinary support when he leaves here so...' He looked at me from underneath those long eyelashes and his dimple twitched as he grinned. His hair flopped over to one side and I thought perhaps we should get a room after all.

'I'll ask Natalia if she might fancy staying over then shall I?'

As I turned to walk away, Jack flicked me on the backside with a towel that I hadn't noticed he'd been carrying and I squealed. Norman was totally oblivious to the severe flirting that was going on around him as he let out a huge fart which made me really laugh out loud.

'Ssshhh! There's sick animals in here. For goodness sake, have you got no decorum, woman?' He winked at me and held out his hand.

I took it and we walked out into the main reception area. The relief I felt that Norman was

OK, was huge. I would never have forgiven myself should anything have happened to him.

It was 4 a.m. I felt totally exhausted. I stood leaning in to Jack's chest, my arms around his waist, before he pulled away when one of the nurses came out to say that they needed him to do a call out to a horse who was giving birth and was in trouble. He kissed my head before he headed back indoors. Natalia rang for a taxi for me and as I waited, I watched a white feather which fluttered down in front of me, landing by my feet. There were no birds in sight. It was still dark. I looked up to the sky and that very bright star was twinkling away. Maybe miracles do happen after all. I mouthed 'thank you' before I got into the taxi and headed home.

'I OWE YOU an apology...' I started.

'Oh my god, Nell, I'm so sorry...'

Shivani looked a wreck. Her eyes were red and she kept wiping her nose with a tissue.

'He's going to be OK, Shivani. He's going to be OK!'

She ran into my arms and sobbed. I stroked her hair.

'It's OK, hon. He's going to be fine.'

'Oh, Nell, I don't think I'd have ever forgiven myself if he hadn't made it. I've been worried sick. Are you sure he's going to be OK?'

'Yep, Jack said with some love and care, he'll make a full recovery. But I owe you an apology. It wasn't anything you did on purpose. I should have known that and shouldn't have been so hard on you.'

'I don't blame you, Nell. I know how fond of Norman you've become. You talk about him like he's your new boyfriend. Oh and talking about your new boyfriend, you and Jack? What's going on there then?'

'I don't really know. All I do know right now, is that you and I need a cup of tea and some sleep. What a day!'

Chapter Thirty-Five

THE SHRILL RINGING of my phone woke me and made me feel quite discombobulated as I reached out to answer it and at the same time noticed that it was nearly 10 a.m. Shivani must have slept in too. It was no real wonder considering the evening's events.

I smiled when I saw Jack's name pop up on the screen, but then when I remembered everything from the evening before, I shot up in bed, hoping that it wasn't bad news he was ringing with.

'Oh my god, Jack, is everything OK with Norman? Is he OK?' I held my breath.

'Morning, gorgeous, he's absolutely fine. He's had a good sleep and we've given him a light breakfast which he's managed to keep down. He's had a little walk and a wee in the courtyard and hc's sleeping again now. I reckon another day of being like this and he'll be fine to come home tomorrow.'

I breathed out. My shoulders dropped all the

tension I'd been holding in them.

My voice caught in my throat. 'Thank you, Jack, for everything you did last night.'

'Everything?' he asked and I could hear in his husky voice that he wasn't talking at that particular moment about Norman.

My body tingled.

'Yes, everything,' I giggled. 'But particularly looking after Norman. I can never thank you enough for what you did for him.'

'It's funny you should say that. I'm sure I can think of a few things.' His voice was low and sultry and I knew he was smiling and that his dimple would be twitching.

Suddenly, I could hear a commotion in the background. 'I'm sorry, Nellie-bum, but I'm going to have to go. Emergency. I'll pop round when after work. Bye.'

Laying my head back on the pillow, I thought to last night and our shared kisses. Kisses I'd waited over twenty years for. And they were everything I'd dreamt of and more. But what happened now? Where did we go from here?

Getting up and putting the kettle on, I was still in a little daydream when Shivani wandered into the kitchen stretching her arms above her head.

'I heard the phone, is everything OK?' she

asked while biting her nails.

'Yes, he's fantastic.' I smiled.

'And what about Norman?' She winked. 'Any of that coffee going spare?'

I grinned. She knew me so well.

'I want to know *everything*. What the fuck has been going on down here in deepest darkest Dorset?'

There wasn't a lot to tell. I hadn't a clue how to describe what was going on. What I did tell her is how much I had loved Jack all those years ago and how seeing him again hadn't quashed my feelings at all, but that I'd been pushing them aside because of Natalia's claims on him.

Talking of Natalia, I checked my phone and noticed that I'd had a text come through to say that she'd meet me at the beach café at twelve for lunch. That didn't give me much time to get ready. I went to call Norman to get ready to go out, but then remembered that he wasn't there. It was funny how you slipped easily into little routines. I missed him being around. The house seemed empty, as if it had lost some of its heart and soul. It's amazing how quickly an animal becomes part of your family, and right then, I felt like I'd created a new little family of my own. I couldn't wait to get him home and surprised myself by how much I was actually missing him.

CHECKING MYSELF IN the full-length hall mirror, this way and that, before I left the house, I reckoned I would give Natalia a run for her money that day. I put on more make-up than usual, finished off with a slick of peach lip gloss and headed over to the café, making sure I was in plenty of time.

Natalia was there before though. I could see her sat in the far corner, hugging a mug of something hot, her dark lustrous hair dazzling me as always with its shine but this time in a high-up pony tail. She looked up as if she sensed me there. Crikey what a difference in her. Gone were the false eyelashes, and the fake tan, her trademark bright lipstick. Instead of long, garishly painted talons, her nails were shorter and French manicured. She was wearing hardly any make-up apart from maybe a brush of light bronzer, a little mascara and a muted lip gloss.

'Natalia, you look…'

'Dull? Boring?'

'Quite the opposite in fact. You look absolutely stunning.'

'Really?' Her shoulders lifted.

'Really. Can I be honest with you about something?'

'Please do.'

'You don't need all that make-up and falseness, Natalia. You are incredibly beautiful without it.'

'Oh, Nell, what a sweet thing to say.'

'It's true. You look so different. But there's something else about you too. I just can't put my finger on it.'

'I think I'm in love, Nell. But I'm such an awful person.'

'Wow!' I wondered what she was going to say next as a tear slid down her cheek.

I reached out for her hand. 'What's happened?'

'Do you know that my name isn't even fucking Natalia. I've been such a pretentious bitch. I'm reverting back to my original name. Plain old Natalie.'

'Natalie, you could never be plain or old. Look at you today. You're beautiful.'

'Nell, you are so lovely and I've been so awful to you.'

There wasn't anything I could say to that to be honest, so I just stayed quiet.

'When I met Reg, I realised that love could come along and just hit you straight between the eyes. I never believed in love at first sight until then. Reg is wonderful. He's sweet, he's kind, he's fair, he's honest and I adore him. I thought that love was more of a business-type deal. You found someone who on paper would be perfect. Someone rich, with ambition, and if you shared the same interests, I thought that was what the future was about. And that's what I saw in Jack. But he never wanted me.'

Still gobsmacked by her revelation, I only just managed to murmur, 'Coffee, a latte, please' to the young waitress who'd headed over.

'I've seen the way Jack looks at you. I could see it in his eyes the moment I first met you. He's never looked at me that way. He looks at you with such admiration and adoration and I could never compete with that. You scared the life out of me, Nell. You came along out of the blue and I knew at that point that I'd lost the future I thought I wanted. But that's all it was. It was never real. There was no planned wedding. I've never even kissed him, well not in a romantic way. Jack told me once that he thought of me as his little sister and that really hurt because I thought that we could have had a good future together. But now I've met Reg, I know that you can't build the future on material things and qualification. It's built on love and respect for each other and that little jittery feeling that I get in my tummy every time I see him. And I think that's what you feel when you see Jack. Am I right?'

I could do nothing else but nod. I dipped my head to the table.

'Then, Nell, please forgive me. I tried to warn you off, but I was so very wrong to do that. I can see that you and Jack have a shared history as well as something very, very special. He told me recently that you were the one who got away. That he loved you dearly when he was a teenager and wanted there to be more between you, but he didn't think you could cope with everything you had going on in your life at the time with your family splitting up. He told me that he just needed to show you that he was your friend and that in time, it would turn into something more, but he never got the chance because you left. He said that he was heartbroken.'

I couldn't take it all in. So, he did like me back then, maybe even felt the same way I'd felt about him.

'Jack told me that you are a really good person, Nell. That you always have been and that you always will be. I am truly sorry for how I've treated you since you arrived here. I hope you can find it in your heart to forgive me and that one day we can be friends. But if you can't, I couldn't ever blame you. What I do know, is that love can make you feel wonderful and loved and amazing.

Protected and safe. And that's how Reg makes me feel and it was different to how I felt about Jack. But it's how I think that Jack feels about you. Don't waste that. I don't think a love like this comes around many times and when it does, I reckon you have to grab it with both hands and see where it takes you. It could be to the most wonderful of places. I'm going to see where it takes me and Reg. And I think that you should do the same.'

She stood to go. I heard the door chime behind me. Natalia smiled at whoever had just walked in. She hesitated as she passed me and laid her hand on my shoulder.

'Go get your man, Nell. You deserve him and all the happiness in the world. You belong together and you belong here in Muddleford. I hope you'll stay forever.'

I turned to watch her walk towards Reg, and she beamed as she took the hand that he reached out to her. As I looked past them both, I noticed that the person who Natalie patted on the arm, reached up and kissed on the cheek and was staring at me from across the room was Jack. My gorgeous, kind, wonderful Jack.

Epilogue

JACK LOOKED ABSOLUTELY gorgeous in his pale-blue three-piece suit. He ran his fingers though his floppy hair and brushed it out of the way of his eyes. I loved that his hairstyle hadn't changed in over twenty years and that that action was now a habit that would never change.

As I walked down the aisle, his eyes held mine, and he smiled that lopsided cheeky grin. I knew that he truly loved me. I could feel it in my heart. I can't believe I ever doubted him. He stood at the front of the church, the vicar bending towards him to quietly speak.

Jack wrung his hands, and tapped his feet, his big moment to shine.

'Best man, do you have the rings, please?'

'I do,' he placed them on the cushion offered.

Reg grinned at him. Jack patted him on the back.

After all the formalities were complete, the vicar announced, 'You may now kiss your bride.'

Reg kissed Natalie gently but full on the lips and dipped her backwards. She giggled and then pulled herself upright, grinning as she turned to look at me after I straightened out her bridal train.

'Thank you for being my chief bridesmaid, Nell.' She squeezed my hand. She looked absolutely stunning today, natural make-up, nothing false about her at all. She made a beautiful, radiant bride.

THE WEDDING RECEPTION took place at the Cock Inn. And yes, Jack and I were still giggling about that name, especially when in his best man's speech, he said that there would definitely be some 'cock in, in the honeymoon suite tonight.'

Val came over and joined us at our table as Jack and I watched everyone around us. We were both people watchers and were having fun, making up our own stories about the party goers. Jack headed off to the bar to get his mum a drink.

'Thanks again, Val, for clearing everything up for me and sharing what you knew about why Mum and Aunty Lil had fallen out.'

'Well, I'm sorry I was the one who had to tell you. I wish that we'd all done more all those years ago to sort it out properly and I should have interfered more to make that happen.'

'Please don't worry. Hindsight is a wonderful thing.'

When I met up with Val, a couple of days after the swishing event, she told me that the night of the argument, Aunty Lil had shouted at Mum and told her that she needed to get help, that she was an alcoholic, that she had wrecked her own life and if she wasn't careful she was going to wreck mine too. She had told Mum that Dad had left her because of her drinking and yet she still couldn't see it.

At this point, Mum apparently still would not admit that there was an issue at all and said that Dad was a womanising narcissist who only ever thought of himself. Mum called Aunt Lil an interfering old bitch and told her to stay out of her life and my life. She said that her daughter was dead and she couldn't replace her with me. Aunty Lil was devastated, apparently, and Mum told her that she wanted nothing to do with her ever again.

Val had been there at the time and heard the whole thing and that's why she knew everything that had happened.

'I really do wish I'd done more, but Lilian told me that it was your mum's decision and that I wasn't to interfere. So I didn't. I'm so happy that everything worked out so well now, although I do wish you'd have got to see Lilian and spent time with her as an adult. And I really am so glad that the stones and the messages helped to get you and Jack on the right track.' She smiled at me. 'I thought you'd never get there under your own steam. What a pair you are!'

'Stones and messages?' I was confused.

'Yes, dear. I felt you and Jack were never going to sort yourselves out. You were dithering about staying here or not, and he wouldn't tell you how he felt. I could have bashed your heads together. That's when I thought that you needed a helping hand. I dreamt one night that Lil and I were painting stones together and it felt like a message from her to do exactly that. You nearly caught me painting them one day in the kitchen and I had to pretend they were cupcakes.'

'Oh my god, Val. You sneaky thing.'

'You think? Not as sneaky as when I had to let myself into the house with my spare key and hide notecards in the pockets of Lil's clothes for you to find.'

My mouth gaped open and she winked as Jack returned and handed her a gin and tonic.

'Got you to the right place though, didn't it? I am so happy that you two are together now. I honestly couldn't be more delighted and I know that Lil would be smiling down on you right now.'

Les joined her and shook Jack's hand before he sat down.

'Mum. Dad. Do you mind if I take Nellie-bum, somewhere? Will you be OK?'

'Of course, son.' His dad gave him a hug. I did love it when men weren't frightened to show their emotions.

We'd grabbed a taxi from the wedding reception and as we arrived back in Larkspur Lane, Jack took my hand and led me down to the beach hut, where he opened it up, went to the fridge and took out a bottle of champagne and brought it over to where I was standing in the entrance.

'I think we deserve this, don't we?'

The moon disappeared briefly behind a cloud, but still, the light shimmered on the sea. It was beautiful here at night, so peaceful, and it filled my heart with joy. I remembered back to the many nights when we were fourteen, when Jack and I used to sneak out of our houses and spend time on the beach, sitting side by side, his leg pressing into mine, making my heart beat that little bit faster, just staring at the sea and the moon for hours on end.

Jack bent down to pick something up off the

floor and tumbled to one side. He righted himself and I realised that he was down on one knee.

I gasped.

'Marry me, Nellie-bum. We've wasted twenty years. Let's not waste a moment longer. Will you marry me?'

Tears streamed down my cheeks as I nodded my head, tried to say yes, and laughed, all at the same time and made a hiccuppy-burpy sound. Trust me to spoil a perfect moment. Jack laughed and woohooed really loud! He threw a blanket over his arm, took my hand in his, grabbed the bottle of champagne in the other and we walked hand in hand down to the sand. We fell to the ground and he kissed me first tenderly, then more passionately. Oh how I loved this man.

He wrapped the blanket around our shoulders and we sat, side by side, his leg pressing into mine, making my heart beat a whole lot faster, and as the moon came out from behind a cloud, and as the brightest star in the sky beamed down on us, we watched the moonlight over Muddleford Cove.

A letter from Kim

I do hope you enjoy your trip to Muddleford.

Muddleford is a fictional seaside place, based upon Mudeford in Dorset where my sister and I spent a great deal of our childhood at our Aunty and Uncle's house where our gorgeous Nan used to take us for the summer holidays. We have so many happy memories and it was lovely to revisit Mudeford in this book.

If you did enjoy Moonlight Over Muddleford Cove, and would like to keep up to date with my latest releases, you can sign up at the following link. Your email address will never be shared and you can unsubscribe at any time.

Sign up here!

www.kimthebookworm.co.uk

I loved writing this book and really do hope you love it too. If you do, I would be super grateful if you were able to leave an Amazon review. It doesn't have to be a huge essay, just a line or two is great too. It really makes a difference helping new readers to discover my books for the first time.

I love to hear from my readers, so do please get in touch.

www.kimthebookworm.co.uk
www.facebook.com/KimtheBookworm
www.twitter.com/KimtheBookworm
www.instagram.com/Kim_the_Bookworm

Acknowledgments

First, I'd like to say a huge thank you to Lauren once more for your editorial advice. Your hard work is much appreciated.

To Radhika, for holding my hand through the final part and doing all the technical stuff.

To Lisa/Mary Jane for creating yet another stunning cover and to Lydia for being my sounding board.

To the awesome Jessica Redland who helped me brainstorm titles when I hadn't a clue what to call this book.

To the blogger and author community that I chat to on a daily basis. I cannot tell you how much you mean to me and have spurred me on to keep writing. Your kind and funny comments, tweets, posts are an absolute joy.

To Audra, this is to make sure that you read the acknowledgements and have a little smile when you read this. Thanks for all your messages about my books and for loving my books. And for forgiving me for telling you to "shut the f*ck up" when I was trying to read on my holidays a million years ago when you kept talking to me! LOL! Sending love to you matey.

To Emma, for the rants on our daily dog walks. Not sure how I'd have coped if I didn't have you to rant to. And we never ran out of words did we?

To Liza, what a year you've had! You've shown bravery, courage, tenacity and determination beyond words. I'm so proud of you and have loved our little bubble and the laughs we've had along the way. And the tears too. So good to have you by my side through this shitstorm of a year.

To all my awesome Bookouture colleagues and authors. To Angie Marsons, Patricia Gibney and Carol Wyer for checking in on me to make sure I'm ok if you don't hear from me for a while. Thanks for caring.

To my book club pals. I've missed you so much this year and can't wait to get back to "what was it called?" and "who was the author again?" And to Kate, our funny, bubbly, lovely book club pal, that Covid took away. Hope you've found the library in heaven Kate. You will be missed.

To Dawn for doing the very first read and let me breathe a sigh of relief.

And finally, to Ollie and Roni. I love you both to the moon and back.

And yes Ollie, I do love you more than you

love me. It's now in a book, in writing, so it's the truth! And I grew you so that gazumps everything. You know it! Thanks for being my lockdown buddy this year. It's been such an honour to spend all this extra time with you.

Love you my fabulous boy xxx

Printed in Great Britain
by Amazon